MW01002097

HUGH HOWEY LIVES

DANIEL ARTHUR SMITH

HUGH HOWEY LIVES

ISBN-10: 978-0988649385

ISBN-13: 0988649381

Edited By
Crystal Watanabe

Cove and Illustrations By
Ben Adams

Also Written by Daniel Arthur Smith

The Cameron Kincaid Adventures
The Cathari Treasure
The Somali Deception

Literary Fiction
The Potter's Daughter
Opening Day: A Short Story

Horror Fiction
Agroland

Science Fiction
Hugh Howey Lives

~*~

For Susan, Tristan, & Oliver, as all things are.
&
To Hugh Howey – This story is a homage to him.

~*~

ONE

There was plenty of wind, and Tia wanted speed to cut through the chop. She swept her long black braid back over her shoulder and gave the winch a vigorous crank. After a series of clacks, the bow lifted, then dipped hard starboard, plowing through the foamy crest of the next wave. Seawater sprayed over the side of the boat and doused the cockpit. Tia shielded her face from the salty froth and then went to the hatch excited to tell Kay they were close. She tilted her head sideways into the cabin. "We're almost there."

"Can you see the island?" Kay asked.

"Come topside and see for yourself."

"Okay," Kay said. "I'm coming. Just let me stow my book." With both hands she carefully closed the precious hardcover she had been reading, wrapped it in the special blue silk cloth Tia gave her two birthdays back, and then tucked the package into the matching blue pouch. She pulled herself up out of the bunk, dipping her knees in sync with the next deep roll. "I thought you said the storm was moving out."

"It was supposed to be," Tia said. "Hurry up. We're almost there."

Tia plopped back in the cockpit near the tiller and grabbed her old camera from its weatherproof case.

Half in, half out of the hatch, Kay braced herself. She

pulled the zipper of her yellow parka higher toward her neck. Strands of brown hair, loose from her ponytail, blew wildly up and around her round apple cheeks and forehead.

Tia wrinkled her nose and snapped two quick shots with the camera. Kay mirrored the cringe, and then turned her head leeward to the fast moving water. "We're really heeling!"

Tia reached her hand out again, fingers spread wide. "Come sit next to me."

Kay climbed out of the cabin and slid down into the cockpit with Tia.

Kay extended her neck to peer beyond the bow. "Is that it?"

"That's your island," Tia said. She raised the camera to photograph Kay's profile against the mountain island jutting from the sea.

"Wow. It's real," Kay said. "And inhabited. See? You thought we'd be lucky if the island was anything more than a rock. But those are turbines."

"Sure are, two of them. One's not spinning though, must be out of service, whatever they powered probably doesn't need them anymore. Means the island is probably abandoned."

"Makes ya think."

"What?"

"Is there any place on this planet Elleron hasn't touched?"

Tia shrugged her forehead. Her last name was synonymous with turbines, new energy, and wealth. Where others failed in wind turbines, her great-grandfather did well. Her father ran the company now. In that way, they were different, Tia and Kay. The entirety of Kay's youth was spent in one of the ten thousand anonymous prefab boxes that rowed the outskirts of New Miami, while Tia's was split between a Georgian riding school, the slopes of the Alaskan Riviera, and the family sailboat. The one they were on today. While Kay read about an ocean far across the city, an ocean unseen, Tia learned to sail amidst the family's turbine farms, learned to tack between the massive columns of those slow spinning titans rising from the sea.

Tia gestured to Kay's right. "Lift that cushion." Kay lifted the top of the seat. "Grab an orange thermos."

"Which one?"

"Doesn't matter, they're both the same. I brought a treat."

Kay reached in and handed Tia one of the cylinders. "Nice. You scored some of that cheap sake from the dorms?"

"Close. It's home brewed ale. I figured we'd need some."

Tia opened the thermos and poured a small amount of the chocolate-colored liquid into the lid. "Here, sip this."

"This is special. I haven't tasted ale in forever. Is this your father's?"

"He made it." Saying he made it was really saying someone in the kitchen made the brew, but they both understood.

"Tastes nutty," Kay said, "he must toast the hops."

Tia sipped from the thermos, then wiped her mouth with the back of her hand. Kay was right; the ale *was* nutty and sweet. She always noticed these things.

Kay drew a second sip from her lid, her eyes traced the mast to the top of the main sheet. "The sail is so full," she said.

"The water is rough, but it's a good day to be out. Better than yesterday."

Kay nuzzled her shoulder against Tia. "I want to sail the world with you."

"With me or with one of your books?"

"I was just checking the coordinates in the hardcover."

"So you're sticking to it? You think that book of yours is going to lead you to Hugh Howey?"

"I'm telling you, we're going to find him on that island. The book says so. It's called *The Island,* Tia. *The Island,* I mean, c'mon. I figured it out. We're going to find him."

"You're ridiculous. It's just another Archive-generated

book, like every other book, and that island is on every geocom. There's nothing special about it, probably just another old resort that shuttered when the water rose. I'm only out here because…" she paused and leaned back. Then, rather than say another word, raised her camera to snap yet another picture of Kay with the island in the background.

"Because it was an excuse to take out the boat," finished Kay.

Tia gave Kay a knowing smile, but she was thinking something entirely different. True, she needed little excuse to go sailing. But she was thinking Kay couldn't let this go, this Hugh Howey thing. That's why they were here in search of the island. Kay was certain, obsessed. A wild sparkle appeared in her eyes whenever his name came up, a pensive nowhere stare that only reared itself when she was writing, or thinking, of him. Tia blamed the Librarian. The Librarian planted the seed of the island, convinced Kay it was so.

"If there's nothing special about this island," Kay asked, "then why would that new book, *The Island,* have his name on the cover?"

"It has his name on the cover so people like you will spend a week's worth of credit on an expensive paperbound book from that antiquated dungeon of a Library, rather than stream it from the Archive like everyone else. I don't get why you hang out in the basement anyway. The place is creepy, and so is the Librarian."

"It's called a Library and the Librarian can print off any book I want in like two minutes. Paper's not cheap, but it's worth it. Way better than what you read."

"Hey, ease up. What I read is fine; puzzles are good for the mind. Besides, that Librarian is creepy, and you know it."

"That Librarian happens to agree with me. He says Hugh has been hiding out on an island for years."

"Does he say that every time you plop down another week's credit?"

"That's not how it is. We talk about Hugh." Kay's

shoulders sunk, and she slid down in her seat. "He says my writing reminds him of Hugh. He promised to help get me a named place in the Archive. You know how hard that is?"

Tia put her arm around Kay and squeezed her. "You've made your way through the university on full scholarship. That is hard. You've won every award the school has to offer, and that is hard, and your professor, what's her name —?"

"Wells."

"Professor Wells says you're a guarantee for the university's genius award in literature. So I'm sure you'll have a place in the Archive regardless of the Librarian. You're as good as Hugh ever was."

"He's better than good. And that award is just an academic thing."

Tia sucked in a deep breath. "Tell me again why you think he picked this island?"

"Well, everyone knows he sailed his catamaran around the world uploading stories to the Archive as he went."

"And then a hundred fifty years ago, give or take, he disappeared, and no one has seen him since."

Kay thumbed a wisp of hair from her eyes. "Right, yet his books keep coming out."

"Books with his name on them, but the math doesn't work, does it? He'd be like… two hundred years old."

Kay dropped her eyes from Tia, sipped her ale, ran her tongue across her lips, and then faced the bow, wincing at the light salty spray. "It's so exciting to be sailing where Hugh Howey sailed," she said.

Tia bit her lower lip. Kay was deflecting. She tried again. "He sailed everywhere." That didn't come out much better.

"But he sailed *here* a lot," Kay said. "He writes about sailing in seventy-three of his stories and most of them involve this area."

"Let me guess. Those are all of the newer books."

"That's right, a lot of his stories are set in islands, and

the latest is titled *The Island*."

"You mentioned that."

Kay scrunched her nose. "And do you know why that is?"

Tia's eyes went wide, "Because the Archive wrote it?"

"Blasphemy." Kay grinned.

At least she's in good humor this time, thought Tia.

"The Librarian agrees with me, you know. Plus, it's a fact that of the three hurricanes he sailed through, two were here. The other was technically a monsoon."

"No one has ever sailed through a hurricane, much less three."

"Hugh did. Fact. You can ask the Librarian when we get back, or better yet, you can ask Hugh yourself."

Tia sucked in a deep breath. "Okay, sure, maybe Hugh did, but I don't want to sail through one. The storm's closer than it's supposed to be so we'll have to find safe harbor at the island." They both peered to the far horizon. A wall of grey melted into the sea below and black clouds above. "We should make it before the visibility drops and, fortunately for us, there's a deep lagoon on the geocom. But you have to promise that when you see he's not there, you're going to let it go."

"I promise," Kay said, "but he's there."

~*~

TWO

Tia bolted the hatch, scanned the deck one last time, and then hopped from the sailboat to the wooden dock. Kay busied herself noting their arrival on her tablet and appeared to pay no attention as Tia checked the lines at the cleats a final time.

"It just means that the resort was probably abandoned more recently than I thought," Tia said.

"What's that?"

Kay could play coy, pretend to hide her pleasure in discovering the dock and the huge building up the mountainside, but Tia saw through her.

Tia gave the last knot a tight yank. "The dock was probably built for the caretaker."

"Of the resort?"

"Yeah. The resort."

With the exception of the giant wind turbines, the island appeared like any other in this part of the world, the near-barren rock of a mountaintop high enough to not be submerged when the Earth's waters rose a hundred years before. Still, they were both surprised when they entered the lagoon. Not only was there the dock, but a bowl canyon that ascended up to the island's summit, and within that hidden hollow, a dense canopied rainforest. Rainforests were not unheard of here – they were in the tropics, after all – but the curvature of the canyon walls all but hid the safe harbor and its surroundings from the outside world. Tia understood why someone decided to build the huge structure up near the summit, as it was the ideal location for a resort, and that's what she decided it was, an old resort, a throwback to a different time. But there was no dissuading Kay.

When Tia shouldered her pack, Kay stopped writing. "Are we ready?"

Tia nodded. "Sails stowed, lines tied. Thanks for asking."

"All right." Kay cupped her tablet, lifted her pack, and headed toward the wide set of wooden stairs that ascended into the rainforest. "I want to make it up there before it rains," she said.

Tia rolled her eyes and shifted her attention to the lens of her old analog camera, squinting to see if the glass was clear. "I guess you feel better," she said loudly.

Kay was already bounding up the steps. "Much!"

"I gotta give it to you," Tia yelled. "From the geocom, I'd have guessed the island was empty! You know that's usually the case with these old places! I mean, the building doesn't even register!"

"No, I told you we'd find Hugh's island and we did!"

Tia frowned. "We found *an* island!" She tilted her head up. The clouds were racing in, a super cell. In her regular voice she added, "And good thing, because that storm shifted for sure."

Kay pointed up the mountainside to the domed roof curving above the treetops. "There's proof," she confidently called down. "That's a hurricane-sheltered manor house, same as the one described in *Lexica!*"

"*Lexica?*"

"Oh, it's a wonderful story about a community that lives in the side of a mountain through a five-hundred-year hurricane!"

"A five-hundred-year hurricane?"

"Uh huh!"

"You know that's impossible, right?" Tia spun around to briefly take in the lagoon, snap a photo, and then continued up. Kay was moving farther ahead, but that was okay.

"Hugh explains it very well. The children are born in vats and have to develop their own language from clues in the complex. It's a parable full of metaphors."

"I was talking about the hurricane. Anyway, the Archive can't write parables."

"Exactly."

Tia peered into the rainforest. Kay could continue the discussion without her help. The beautiful botanicals were far more interesting than another '*Hugh Howey lives*' debate. The university's botanical garden, where she worked, held a sliver of flora compared to the rainforest surrounding her. This place was different than any Tia had ever visited or even seen. The canopy above was flooded with the chirps of countless birds, and the muted light of the clouded grey sky brought out an array of deep green hues from the lush broad leaves surrounding the stairwell. At every landing, she stopped to shoot yet another photo of the shadowed undergrowth or the rapidly fogging vista. She spotted several peach and coral torch gingers blooming near the base of the trees, each blossom comprised of a hundred thin, tightly packed petals. As they ascended, the air thickened with moisture and the pungent scent of the many floral variations, more varieties here in one small area, she realized, than all of those at the botanical gardens combined.

After shooting photos off a high landing, she turned to climb the next flight of stairs and then froze. Off to the right, almost unnoticeable from the walkway, a half dozen white orchid blooms wrapped their tendrils around the base of a tree. Tia recognized the white orchid. Any botanist would. *Dendrophylax lindenii*, the ghost orchid. Not once did even Ms. Barnes, the lead professor at the university garden, ever see a ghost orchid in the wild. Ms. Barnes told her that ghosts in the wild were rare, possibly extinct, like most strains obsolete to those bred in the nursery. *Extinct in the wild, like Kay's authors.* Tia snickered at the thought. Authors weren't extinct. Authors were obsolete, just as Hugh predicted they would be a hundred and fifty years ago. At least, Kay said he'd predicted it. *Maybe that's why Kay's fixation on Hugh was so strong,* Tia thought. Kay was an author in the wild. All she wanted was to have people read her stories, the way she thought they once read Hugh's. Tia tried to explain to her why the Archive's books were just better for everybody, tailored to fit the reader. But then, she worked in a botanical garden. How could she tell her lover that there was any difference between the beauty of flowers and the beauty of words? How could a designer orchid be as beautiful as these rare ghosts, hiding in their glade? She lifted her camera and played with the lens. A large drop of water landed on her forehead and trickled into a rivulet down the side of her face. She raised her hand to wipe the water away. Another drop fell on her shoulder, and then another.

"Are you coming?" Kay yelled down from the top of the steps. "It's starting!"

Tia waved and pointed at her camera, an attempt to seduce Kay into one final pose before the rain came.

~*~

THREE

Halfway up the mountainside, the first of the storm cells darkened the already grey sky. There was no gradual change in precipitation, instead there was a rapid wave of an oncoming mist, a few heavy drops, and then each ascending step became a wall of water as sheets of rain pressed into the island. A rushing creek replaced the dirt path that ran alongside the wooden stairs, and when Tia and Kay, drenched hood to shoe, finally reached the highest landing, water columns were weaving across the stone patio in torrents and blurring their view of the large manor's facade. They ran toward the huge brown wooden door and the shelter of the patio's awning, a glassed section of the domed rooftop that drooped down in a 'V' to the front of the manor. They shook the wet from their parkas and Kay reached for the large metal knocker, a huge bulbous brass pendant on the upper middle of the door, and slammed it against its metal backplate.

"What if there's no one here?" Tia asked. Kay's eyes bored into her.

They didn't have to wait to see. The door swung open to reveal the face of a man.

"You made it up. Come in, come in." He removed himself from blocking the door so that the two could enter. A wall of cool air met them as they entered a huge hall, where the ceilings were high and vaulted, and on either end were parlors with small sitting areas. The hall reminded Tia of the grand lobbies in the resorts she had visited with her family. The man was well-dressed in tan linen slacks, loafers, and a pressed collared short-sleeve shirt, appropriate for the island, but not formal or worn, Tia noticed, clothes fresh from a synthesizer. Then the thought swirled that they could be real cotton. If a man could afford an island, he could afford tailor-made cotton clothes, like her father could. The man reminded Tia of her father. He wasn't much older. His hair was greyed on the sides, but not all the way through the top. And the way he smiled at them, two drenched strays dripping pools of rainwater onto the floor of the hall, just like her dad would greet them.

"We saw you make the harbor and had our fingers crossed you'd beat the rain."

"You've been waiting for us?" Kay asked.

"Yes. We pinged your transponder before you reached the island and then verified your craft."

"Of course you did," Tia said.

"Can't be too safe, scavengers and all." He bit his lip and then added, "Excuse me, I'm Bill. Bill Deming."

"Nice to meet you, Bill," Tia said. "I'm Tia Elleron."

Kay dropped her pack from her shoulder and took Bill's hand into her own. "Hi," she said. "I'm—"

"Kay Milan," Bill said.

Kay slowly tilted her head to the side. "How did you know that?"

"Oh, I'm sorry. Your name was registered on the transponder with Miss Elleron." He chuckled awkwardly. "Welcome to our little island."

"Oh. Of course," Kay said. She let her hand fall awkwardly to the side. "Thank you."

"Tia, please," Tia said. "Thank you for the hospitality."

Tia took in the museum-quality furnishings decorating the room, the pieces were as familiar to her as were the periods they were from. The rainbow-colored glass chandelier she wasn't sure about. She would ask Kay later. Kay would be able to identify each one. She raised her arms from her sides and looked down at her soaked capris and sneakers, and the small pool gathering on the woven carpet. "Sorry," she said, pulling her neck taut. "I guess we kinda barged in."

"Don't be absurd. You two are lucky. That storm has done an about face. I'm glad we were here."

Tia eased her pack from her shoulder. "So you don't mind if we ride the storm out with you?"

"Not at all. We have plenty of room. One minute." Bill turned his head toward the wide mahogany stairwell at the back of the hall. "Sebastian! We have guests." He smiled at Kay and Tia again. "Sebastian will be here in a moment to show you to a room."

"You said we, is it just the two of you? You and Sebastian?"

"Oh, no," he said. "There are ten of us here. You'll meet the others at dinner. And Sebastian is—"

Bill stopped himself midsentence and glanced up toward the wide flight of mahogany stairs. On the landing above, a towering figure silhouetted the large decorative stained glass mandala.

At first Tia saw only the tall man's blonde hair and the light sport coat he wore, but then as he descended the stairs, she realized he wore coveralls underneath. "I see," she said. "Sebastian is a syn."

"Yes," Bill said. "Sebastian is a synthetic Model Nine."

The Model Nine was old when Tia was a girl. Her grandfather owned a Model Nine manservant named Claude. Like all models since, the Model Nine syns were designed to closely resemble humans. They were very passible, but easy to distinguish as syns without the bioderm layered skin of the new models. Their hair, regardless of color, was fine, too fine, like silk. The colored sclera of their eyes glowed from subtle LED backlights, and their vinyl skin, a breakthrough in movement and flexibility at the time, lacked the full mobility of the later models that more closely mimicked humans.

"Sebastian—and a few others—help out quite a bit

around here," added Bill. "Don't you, Sebastian?"

Sebastian turned his head toward Bill and responded in the genteel manner of the Model Nine. His voice was calm and smooth, and his mouth, chin, and lips moved in the mildest mimic of word pronunciation, despite being vinyl, not bio. "We aim to please, sir."

Tia thought that if she squinted, if she could tone down those brilliantly blue eyes, he might look like a real man.

"Of course," Bill said. "Sebastian. This is Miss Tia and Miss Kay. They will be staying in the Lassiter Suite. Could you please escort them there?"

"Certainly. May I take your…" Sebastian's head pivoted on his neck to take inventory of whatever they may have brought with them, "bags."

The girls picked up their packs. "No. That's all right."

Sebastian's vinyl mask was limited in expression, yet the fluid way he rolled his head in time with his forearm to gesture back toward the staircase was as inviting as any smile. "This way, please."

"Please feel free to relax and enjoy the estate," Bill said, "and I'll see you both at dinner."

"Thank you," they each said.

They followed Sebastian two flights up the grand staircase. From the stairs he led them through a gallery, a small part of which opened to the grand hall they had entered through. Tia looked down. Bill was not there. "The chandelier?" she whispered. "Chihuly, the twentieth century glass sculptor," Kay answered. Tia placed her right hand on Kay's shoulder. Dependable Kay. Further along, a corridor led off to another wing.

"This place is endless," Kay whispered into Tia's ear.

Tia nodded. "It sure is."

"Just like in *Lexica*."

Tia pretended she didn't hear, but Kay was right about the size. The corridor revealed the manor to be even deeper than it was wide. The manor estate was huge.

Tia recognized the paintings adorning the corridor, or at least the artists by their style. They were more modern than the furnishings in the entry hall.

Sebastian stopped, turned, and raised his arm into an open doorway. "The Lassiter Suite."

The two walked past him into the suite, a large apartment-sized room with a sofa, café table, chairs, and two large beds canopied with decorative mosquito netting. The back of the room was a full windowed wall with sliding glass doors that opened to a balcony.

"This place is so big," was all Kay said.

"It is," Tia said. She learned not to comment too much on things such as the size of rooms. Their upbringing was too different. She looked back at Sebastian, who was waiting in the corridor. "Thank you, Sebastian."

"Will Miss Tia or Miss Kay be needing anything else?"

"No," she said. "You're relieved."

The faint sound of hydraulics could be heard as Sebastian bowed his head forward, and then he was gone. Tia dropped her pack to the floor and went over to the glass wall. The rain was coming down hard. She squinted to see past the heavy torrents. She removed her camera from where she'd tucked it safely beneath her red parka and peered through the lens. She frowned.

"What are you looking at?" Kay asked.

"There seem to be two syns down in the courtyard."

"What are they doing out there?"

"I don't know. My dad says the rain doesn't hurt them." She unzipped her parka. "I just don't know... To treat them like that."

"I wouldn't know. My family could never afford a syn."

So there it was, no matter the reassurance Tia gave her, Kay's insecurity prevailed.

"Oh no," Kay said.

Tia left the window, set her camera down, and slipped her jacket from her shoulders. "What's wrong?"

"My tablet. It's supposed to be waterproof."

"Let me see." Tia took the tablet from Kay, tapped the black screen a few times, and then handed the dead device back. "Your writing's backed up to the Archive, right?"

"Uh huh. But that's the only tablet I have to write in." Kay took the tablet back. "Maybe it's water resistant, not water proof. I mix those up."

~*~

FOUR

When Sebastian led them into the second floor dining room, Tia was immediately taken with the dark mahogany paneling. Even with her rare access to the most exclusive resorts, she never saw a structure so flamboyantly resourced, for so few. Full wooden structures such as the pine log lodges of Aspen were rare. Wood paneling was a flex of wealth of the type that her father and his friends frowned upon. Her family was fortunate to have survived times when wealth was dangerous. It was better to be subtle. That was one of the reasons her father loved the sailboat, *"An excuse to be surrounded by wood,"* he said, *"without flaunting."*

But the paneling was not the only thing special in the room. The far wall to her right, and the arched ceiling above, were paned with the same durable glass-like transparency as the greenhouse walls of the university's botanical garden. The thickness of the panes and the darkness of the night hid the weather beyond in a black void. If not for the heavy rivulets running down the frames and the remote flash of electric cyan that filled the sky when they entered, she would have thought the storm passed. Wide palm fronds sprung from tall corner vases and were positioned high in such a way that they appeared to hold up the ceiling. The centerpiece of the room was the dining table. Though not unique, it was impressive, a long table, mahogany like the paneling, surrounded by a dozen brown high back leather chairs, and in them, their waiting hosts.

Kay leaned into Tia's ear. "It's *The Dining Room*."

"What?"

"*The Dining Room*," she repeated. "It's from another story."

"No, no. I know what—"

"I present Miss Tia and Miss Kay," Sebastian said.

Four men and six women rose from their seats at the table to face the two women. Bill was standing across the table, in the middle. Only he and the silver-haired woman at the far head of the table to the right offered anything close to a smile. The others held expressions that ranged from inquisitive to objectively observant to downright bothered.

A gaunt, grey-haired man raised a cloth napkin to his mouth in a poor attempt to hide his whispers to the younger woman next to him. The woman wore an aubergine ḥijāb over her head. She was one of the group peering at the two girls with a bothered stare. Tia was sure the comment was about her and Kay's appearance. Everyone at the table was dressed for dinner. Tia and Kay were in light blouses and capris. Except for a long-sleeved thermal and some undergarments, that's all they bothered to pack. Tia slid her right foot behind her left. She wanted to drop her gaze toward the floor. Etiquette stopped her.

The silver-haired woman at the head of the table must have sensed her discomfort. "Please, come sit next to me," she said, gesturing to the two empty chairs to her left. "You have to excuse us. It's been so long since we've had visitors." The woman's dark eyes darted a silent scolding to the others at the table, and then went pleasantly back to Tia and Kay.

The message made clear, the others began to smile and nod.

The woman gestured for Kay to take the seat to her left.

"Thank you," Kay said.

Tia nodded as well. She waited behind the second chair for the others to retake their seats. Bill stood next to the woman across from her, and when her eyes met his, she caught his subtle wink and nod, a signal to go ahead and sit. When Tia lowered herself into the chair, the others sat and resumed their conversations. The waft of humanity allowed Tia to breathe a bit easier. She was accustomed to formal dinners, but felt uncomfortable because she and Kay essentially forced their invitation by what her mother would have called *'dropping in unannounced.'* In the back of her mind, her mother and a long list of nannies were making that face between a frown and a smile.

At least Kay was by her side.

Tia may have been raised at these tables, but Kay was far more at ease. After they were seated, Kay placed her right hand onto the hand of the silver-haired woman. "Thank you so much for the hospitality," she said in a calm, soothing tone. "Your house is so beautiful."

"Oh, the—" the woman began to say, obviously taken by Kay.

"The room is wonderful," Kay said, "the bath is wonderful."

The woman appeared, not surprised, but curious, and elated at once. Kay could do that to people, Tia thought. Put them under a spell.

Kay continued, "And we're especially grateful that you let us in without knowing us."

Tia placed her hand on Kay's thigh.

Kay's head pivoted around to catch Tia's waiting smile. "Thank you for helping us," Kay finished softly.

Tia thought the woman's dark eyes were about to tear. The woman was clearly handsome in her youth, and though the hair that must have once been raven black was now silver, her elegance remained. She gazed at Kay for a long moment and then smiled again, slid her hand out from under, and then patted the top of Kay's. "You're quite welcome," she said. "My name is Allegra. Allegra Acardi. To my right is Connie Cortez, Susan Chan. You've met Bill. Next to him are Monica Wynn, and at the end of the table is Hector Vazquez. Across from him is Quentin Mills, Zaynah Ahmad, Walter Cain—"

"Doctor Cain, if you please," the gaunt, grey haired man abruptly said.

The woman next to Tia leaned into her and, in a tone mocking Doctor Cain said, "We're all doctors here. I am Doctor Fukai, but please," she smiled widely, "call me Emma."

"Doctor Cain stands on tradition," added Bill, "and we give him that. The rest of us are a bit more casual. Imagine how monotonous it would be if we all greeted each other on this small island as Doctor." His eyes darted to Allegra. "Would you agree, Doctor?"

Kay let free a giggle, infecting the others around Tia – Connie, Susan, and Emma. Allegra kept decorum, and Tia and Kay composed themselves to follow their host's lead.

"You're all doctors," Tia said. "So this is not a resort?"

"Oh, no," Allegra said. "This is a research station, and as I said before, we don't receive that many visitors."

"I apologize that we came unannounced." There, Tia said it, though Kay already thanked them, the weight was heavy.

"Almost met you with a missile," Doctor Cain said.

"Oh." Tia was unable to hide the alarm on her face.

Allegra frowned. "We've been monitoring your transponder since early this morning. We thought you might be coming to investigate the issues we've been having with one of the turbines."

"We saw one of the turbines was stalled when we arrived, but we didn't see them on the geocom."

"You wouldn't have seen them. We keep the turbines masked from the geocom to avoid attracting scavengers, and only a few restricted Elleron systems monitor their performance."

"And ours was not one of those," Kay said.

"Yet you were in an Elleron craft. Caught us off guard. Initially we were confused as to why a repair craft wasn't announced, or a shuttle flown in, and then when we saw your speed and realized that you weren't a repair corvette, we thought you might be—" Allegra raised her brow.

"A scavenger corsair," Tia said. "Yes, I apologize. I do see the confusion now. You see, we didn't realize you were even here."

Kay shook her head. "I don't understand the confusion. You thought we were a repair ship because of our transponder?"

"Our boat's transponder and our geocom are in the company's name," explained Tia. "We appear on geocom as an Elleron craft. Scavengers use sailing corsairs to go undetected in open water and often use stolen transponders to get near an occupied area."

"You're lucky our defense system didn't kick in," Doctor Cain muttered, "you shouldn't be out so far."

"Again, we're sorry," Tia said. "Thank you for your hospitality."

Allegra peered bitterly toward Doctor Cain, and then said kindly, "To have you and your friend here, even by happenstance, Miss Elleron, is a treat for us all."

Bill raised his glass of wine. "Here, here. To new friends."

The others raised their glasses, waited for Tia and Kay to do the same, and then a cascade of "Cheers" rounded the table.

"This is lovely," Tia said, and sipped more red wine from her glass.

"Thank you," Hector said from the end of the table. "I grow the grapes myself, on the south slope."

Kay added, "It's different than any wine I've ever tasted. The aromas are lovely. The bouquet is fascinating."

"Be careful," Connie said. "If you encourage him, he will be forced to tell you that it's the soil carried on the wind from Africa." She moved her right hand slowly across her plate, fluttering her fingers.

Kay lifted her glass to see into the wine. "That's what adds that dirt pie aftertaste." And Tia was certain she meant it.

Susan held her forearm at forty-five degrees. "If you ask, he'll tell you it's the angle of the south slope that adds the hint of fruit."

Tia sipped from her glass again. She tasted the soil she did not notice before. She was raised around fine wine yet only could tell the difference by color. Her Kay was a self-taught connoisseur, an autodidact in all things.

"I think it's great you make your own wine," Kay said. "You'd be challenged to find any real wine at the university. We only have cheap sake at best."

Hector shrugged. "We are rather self-sufficient here. My colleagues are right, though, I know everything about Connie's kumquats, and she in turn knows the secrets of my vines."

"Well, I still think this is nice."

"Then you won't be disappointed here," Doctor Cain said. "Perhaps Miss Elleron can tell us what she and her friend are doing so far out. With the current weather, this is a two-day sail from New Miami. Not a very safe distance with scavengers about, and the storm."

"A pleasure cruise, really," Tia said. "The storm was supposed to be going out, and I didn't think about scavengers."

Three syns, Model Seven servers, smaller and more petite in design than Sebastian, entered from the side of the dining room. They each carried a covered serving tray. In unison, they placed the trays on the table, removed the lids, and began to serve.

"Though we still take the necessary precautions, scavengers haven't been seen in these parts in years," Allegra said. "But the storm is a real concern. I'm afraid you'll be our guests for the next few days."

"Really," Kay said. "That long?"

"Your boat will be safe in the lagoon. You won't want to go out on the open water though. You can contact your family to let them know you'll be all right. Apart from that, I'm afraid we don't connect to the outside, unless there is true emergency."

Kay frowned.

"It's because of our research," added Allegra. "You understand, of course."

"Believe me," Kay said. "This is a great place to be

holed up, it's just that…"

"Just what, dear?"

"Kay's tablet fell victim to the rain," Tia said, "and she was hoping to access her backup in the Archive."

"No problem," Bill said. "We have access to the Archive. You're free to use one of our tablets in the library."

"You have a library?" Kay asked.

"Certainly," Bill said, "actually, that's the kind of research we do in the Calypso Project. We work in publishing."

"I knew it," Kay said.

"Knew what, dear?" Allegra asked.

Tia smiled. "Kay has this crazy idea that Hugh Howey lives out here, and is still writing books. Can you imagine that, Hugh Howey alive, writing books?"

Conversation at the table stopped. Allegra's face became stern, her peering eyes fixed toward, almost through her, in an intense glare. Tia realized she said something terribly wrong.

"You said you didn't realize we were even here," Allegra finally said.

"No," Tia said. "We didn't."

"She didn't believe me," Kay said. "I found the clues."

"The clues?" Allegra asked.

A syn placed a bowl of vegetable soup on Tia's plate. "Thank you," she said. "Kay has this idea that this author, Hugh Howey, has left bread crumbs in his books, leading to this island."

Quentin, the round-faced portly man at the end of the table, chuckled aloud and then simply said, "Clues in books."

Allegra looked long at Quentin, nodded slowly, and then

returned to her kind demeanor. "Young people," she said. "You are the future. Let's eat our dinner. Shall we?"

~*~

FIVE

Tia didn't remember walking up to the top of the mountain, but there they were, her and Kay, fingers interlocked, hands swaying forward and back, laughing as they did on their strolls along the New Miami Boardwalk. They weren't on the boardwalk. They weren't in New Miami at all. They'd hiked up beyond the manor, to the top of the island. The mountaintop was lit up by small fires that spat from openings in the rocks around them. The night sky was starless, a blanket of void. Kay was giggling. Tia said something funny. She could not remember what she said. She could not remember saying anything.

That was not all.

Kay's laughter was silent. Everything was silent, except for a faint drumming. Kay's face went blank, and the drumming became louder. It seemed to be coming from all sides. Kay's eyes darted around to find the source. She looked worried. Tia's chest tightened. She squeezed her hand, yet Kay's slipped away. Kay spun to her side, searching, and then to the other. Tia could not move. She could only watch as Kay stepped back. Kay was scanning the night, the darkness. Tia reached for her, to grab her, to keep her from wandering. She swiped, yet her lover was out of reach. Kay froze, and then slowly hunched forward, ready to pounce, as if she sensed

26

something in the darkness that Tia could not see. Tia tried to call out. Nothing. Her jaw was loose, empty.

And then Kay launched herself into the blackness and was gone.

The light of the fires faded, disappeared. Darkness enveloped the flames, enveloped her, held her, pulled her down onto her side. Tia rolled her head to one side, and then to the other, searching for Kay. And then she saw a series of faint blue pulses. She reached out again and this time she felt something, something in the darkness. Warmth. A soft warmth, a surface, the warmth of a sheet, and then as her hand slid up, the edge of a pillow.

She let her eyelids slip open.

A strobe of electric blue filled the suite. Kay, no longer in the bed next to her, was at the window.

The flashes of lightning appeared constant, and the thunder, silent earlier in the evening, was no longer muffled, the glass of the wall in their suite different from that of the dining room.

Tia ran her tongue across her lips in a failed attempt to moisten them, and then with a rasp said, "You're awake."

Kay's stare, the one she wore when writing, was fixed out the glass wall. "I couldn't sleep. It's as if the storm found us and is hovering here."

Tia pushed herself up to her elbow and stretched her right arm toward the bottle of water on the nightstand. She looked for Kay's tablet, curious if she was writing, but it was too dark for her to see. After wetting her mouth, she said, "It just seems like it. This is an island, high ground. We'll be fine."

"Still," Kay said. "It's like one of his books."

"It's too late for that. C'mon back to bed."

"I can't sleep."

"You're still thinking about that library."

"Can you believe how many books they have? Two stories, floor to ceiling, and hardcover, not vending machine printed paperback, *hardcover*. I've never seen so many. Tell me you've never seen so many."

Tia sighed. Apparently, it wasn't too late for this conversation. Of course, Kay was right.

"I've never seen so many either," Tia said. "They're doing publishing research, they have a lot of books."

"But what does that mean, publishing research?"

"I would bet that they are studying algorithms."

"Remember how Bill called it the Calypso Project?"

"Yeah, so?"

"Do you remember the story of Calypso?"

"No. Not really."

"Calypso was a nymph who lived on the island of Ogygia."

Tia replied through a yawn, "Okay."

"Calypso kept Odysseus on that island to make him her immortal husband."

"That's creepy. Come back to bed."

"Did you see how they all froze up when you mentioned his name?"

"Sure." Tia sat up and let her feet drop to the floor. The bamboo flooring was warm, and though she was only in panties and a light shirt, the room was comfortable. "They were probably surprised that you were so quick to see through them."

"What do you mean?"

"Well, experts like to believe they are fooling everybody. They were obviously shocked to discover a reader was able to track them down. I have to admit I thought you were seeing things, but it all makes sense."

Kay turned her head to Tia. "You mean you believe me now? You finally believe that Hugh stopped sailing and set up here?"

"I believe that the Archive starts with seed stories, and that they can only work with the data that's input, rearranging it to create thousands of stories. You said yourself, the longitude, latitude, the island, even the manor has all been reused. You noticed. That's all I'm saying. I'm sure it freaks them out that amount of detail has slipped into the books and if someone reads enough they're able to see the flaw. That's why I like the puzzle books. At least they're straightforward."

Kay shifted her gaze back out to the rain. "I think he's here."

Tia stood up, pressed her body to Kay's back, and then wrapped her arms around her. "I know you do."

She moved Kay's ponytail to the side, kissed her neck, and then rested her chin on her shoulder.

"You're watching the lightning?"

"I'm looking at that glass dome across the courtyard. Somebody is moving around down there."

Tia stretched to peer out. A number of glass buildings that were hidden earlier by the rain were lit in the night, and one of them, a rising bubble across the courtyard, was a large glass dome. It couldn't be missed, a glass-paned structure as high as their room. "I see a couple figures," Tia said. "I'm sure it's the syns. They don't need to sleep, you know."

"I know," Kay said. "I thought that too. But I was also thinking they don't need the light."

"Hmm. You're right. That is odd."

"I want to go see what's going on."

"You want to go snooping around? I'm serious, you need to come back to bed."

Kay spun around, nose to nose with Tia. "C'mon. Let's get dressed." The pitch in Kay's voice was unmistakable. She'd already made up her mind.

Kay gave Tia a quick smooch and then moved toward their clothes.

"I don't think that's a very good idea," Tia said. "We're guests, remember? Uninvited guests. Uninvited guests with nowhere to go in this storm."

Kay grabbed her capris from the other bed and began to wriggle them on. "Well, I'm going."

Tia was certain of that, certain that if Kay were drawn to something, she would have to go. She would go. She was courageous enough to go.

"You're going to get us into trouble," Tia said.

"You know you want to come with me."

There was truth in what Kay said. Tia's upbringing was privileged, but it was also regimented. Her childhood memories were made up of a series of nannies veering her course into the 'correct direction'. Except for Sara, the one caregiver who let her try new things. Kay reminded her of Sara. From the first day they met. Neither of the two came from any such structure. Kay, like Sara, was her own woman. Against odds, she made it out of the outskirts of New Miami and all the way to the university. And she wanted to, no, was going to be, a writer, a vocation no parents, no structured upbringing, would allow.

Tia took her capris from the bed. If Kay was going to go, she wasn't going alone.

~*~

30

SIX

The tiny crystal LEDs that lined the ceiling of the hall glowed the same low amber hue as the small mountaintop fires Tia saw in her dream. The subtle gleam of the lights teased her waking eyes, adding distance to the already long corridor. Her body was still half asleep, and if Kay would've come back to bed, Tia would have drifted off without another thought. Instead, she was pushing herself to keep up, swinging her arms front to back as she walked, pumping them, to keep her stride even with Kay's.

"What's your hurry?" Tia asked in a hushed voice.

"No hurry," Kay said. She slid a sly grin toward Tia, but her eyes beamed forward, locked on her purpose.

"We don't even know where we're going," Tia said. "We haven't gone down this way before."

"This place is decorated like a mansion, but it's really set up like an institution. Right?"

"I guess. I hadn't thought about it." Tia wouldn't have. Kay always let her imagination paint an odd picture. Tia adored that most times.

"I mean it's like a hotel or a university building," Kay said.

"Okay. So?"

"So – there should be another staircase near the end of the hall. All we need to do is look for the door."

"There are a lot of doors."

"But there will be a door at the end, and when we go

31

down, we should be at the side of the courtyard."

Tia's mind was a bit fogged, but that made sense, and at the end of the hall, there were four doors. Without hesitation, Kay went for the closest handle. Tia sucked in a breath and held it as Kay gave it a gentle turn. Tia let the breath out. The door was locked. Kay went to the next. That door opened to stairs.

"See – I told you," Kay said. "C'mon."

"You're lucky we didn't wake anybody…" Kay was already heading down the stairwell. "And you're insane," Tia said, trailing behind.

Two flights down they found a glass door, the entrance to a dark, glass-paned corridor.

"Look," Kay said gesturing to the right. "The dome is over there."

And the dome was to the right, and far more significant at ground level than from their view in the Lassiter suite.

"I really don't think this is a good idea."

Kay spun her head back. "Enough."

Tia wasn't used to being scolded, certainly not by Kay. But this was Kay's thing.

The panes in the corridor were made of the same transparent material as those in the dining room, muffling the thunder. The bright bubble of the dome, and the dim light in the main entry hall on the opposite side of the courtyard, were the only beacons in the darkness, except for when the silent arcs of lightning webbed the sky and strobed the high walls of the Manor in white. Tia peered through the torrents of rain in search of the dark balcony they had left but she couldn't find it. The Lassiter Suite was somewhere in the middle of the large wall, but all of the rooms were dark, indistinguishable. The silhouette of the mountaintop that rose up around them also came into view in the flashes, as well as the other buildings of the compound scattered beyond the corridor. Squinting, she could make out darkened doors, windows, and trees, but nothing else. As they grew closer to the dome, she saw the figures moving around inside. From the bald peach-colored heads, she decided they were syns, as they thought, four of them. They appeared to be pushing tall metal carts into a large white cube in the center of the dome.

The corridor continued beyond the corner of the courtyard on into the night. Tia could not see the end, only darkness. When the flashes came, she could see the huge shadow of another structure through the glass. Kay wasn't interested in where the corridor led. She veered to the right to the adjacent glass hall, and then boldly pushed through a set of double doors to the connected greenhouse that bordered the courtyard. Tia caught the doors as they slapped back. Kay didn't wait for her to catch up. The dome was through another set of double doors on the far side of the room, and they were almost there. Tia was glad that they were walking along the courtyard wall. The greenhouse was dark and full of tall wide plants that appeared to move under the rapid flashes of lightning. Kay seemed not to notice. She didn't stop until she was outside of the double glass doors of the dome.

Tia grabbed her by her upper arm.

"All right," she said. "Now that you can see what's in there, let's go back."

"What do you suppose they're doing?"

"I dunno. Pushing stuff into that storage room."

"Don't you think that's strange? A storage room under a dome?"

"I guess." Tia let loose of Kay's arm. She wasn't sure what she thought was in the cube. Up close, the cube looked huge, at least twenty-feet on all sides, maybe more. She imagined maybe a storeroom with tall shelves full of electronics and stuff, perhaps an elevator bay, which would have made sense.

"There was something like this in *Lexica*," Kay said.

"This isn't a book. They're liable to catch us."

Kay leaned her face into the glass. "No way. Syns don't care about people. They're old Model Sevens, probably won't even notice us walking in. Look, those two are leaving out the side. I bet the other two follow in a second."

Tia guessed Kay's next words before she said them.

"We're going in."

Kay waited for the two syns to leave the cube. This time she grabbed Tia by the arm and leaned her weight on the door. As soon as the two syns left, Kay pushed the doors open and pulled Tia through.

Tia tried to resist but then shuffled her legs to keep up.

The inside of the dome was illuminated bright white. Her eyes followed the curve of the glass-paned wall up to where it disappeared at the top of the cube. She expected to see bedroom lights flicker on across the courtyard as their hosts rallied to round them up, but instead saw only rivers of rain streaming across the panes.

A motion sensor triggered the sliding doors of the huge cube to open.

Kay tugged her inside.

And then they both froze.

She felt Kay's hand let loose go of her arm and fall away.

For a moment everything fell away.

Tia wasn't sure what she was seeing.

The room was square, a cube on the inside as it was on the out.

Silent movies ran across the high sidewalls.

And there, in the center of the room, suspended in a circle of chromed steel, was a man.

His arms reached outward, his legs spread wide, a living depiction of Da Vinci's Vitruvian Man. A low-hung loincloth draped his waist, and a myriad of tubes pushed and pulled fluids in and out of veins and into the tall metal carts the syns wheeled around. From the base of the man's skull a cascade of wires and cables flowed down through holes in the floor. His eyes were closed, but in a restful way. In fact, he did not appear to be stressed at all from his suspension.

Tia recognized the man. Not at first, but then she did.

He had aged, of course he would have. His body was gaunt, his hairline far receded, and what hair was left was white and thin, except that of his beard, which billowed from his chin and cheeks unfettered. Still she recognized him. Age had not changed him much from the image on the back cover of Kay's printed books.

Tia began to speak and then realized she was breathless. She gulped in some air and in one release said, "It's him."

"I know," Kay said softly. "It's Hugh Howey."

~*~

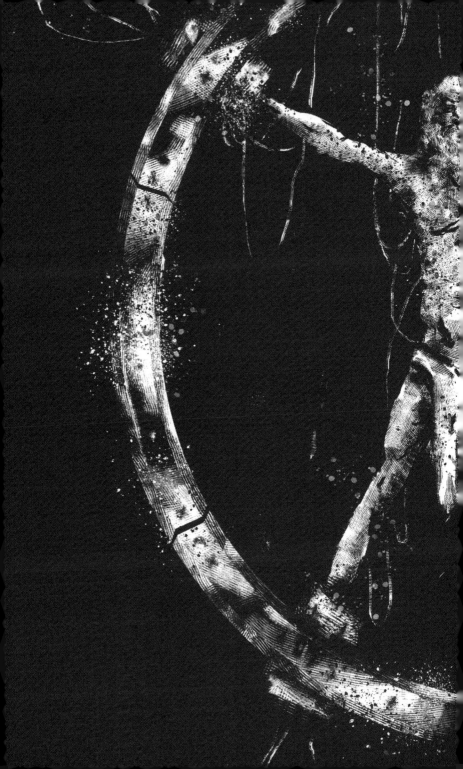

SEVEN

A huge floor-to-ceiling wave washed the left wall, bathing it in aquamarine. Another followed, and then another, and then the image of a ship's bow, ornate with an intricately carved angel figurehead, filled the wall. Kneeling on the foredeck of the old wooden sailboat, fastening hooks to the jibstay, was a svelte young woman in full body wet gear.

Kay elbowed Tia's arm. "That's Cassandra," she whispered.

"Who?" Tia asked.

"Cassandra at sea. She's one of Hugh's characters. She sails around the world in search of adventure." She turned her head toward the wall to the right. "That's Lesley. She lives alone on a space station."

"They're characters?"

"I think so. So is he, on the back wall, the boy flying in the jetpack, that's Billy. He's one of my favorites."

"Are these movies from the books?"

"I dunno. I don't remember Billy ever flying with a jetpack, and I'm sure I've read all of the *Thorne* stories."

"I assure you," said a man from behind. "You haven't read that one."

Startled by the voice, Tia and Kay spun around.

The voice belonged to one of the doctors, the round-faced man who had been seated at the end of the dinner table, far down from Tia. He was wearing a white lab coat and held his hands clasped together in front of him. He rocked slowly on his heels, sizing the girls up.

"Oh," Tia said. "We're so sorry, um, Doctor…" Her mind raced through the faces at the table. "I'm sorry, I forgot your name."

The man smiled. "Doctor Mills. Quentin is fine."

"We were… we just, well, we got lost."

"You got lost?"

Tia nodded.

Quentin looked the two over with a playful eye. "At two in the morning?" He grinned. "I don't think so."

"You don't?" Kay asked.

"It's all right. We were going to bring you down here tomorrow anyway. He wanted to meet you."

Tia and Kay slowly glanced back at the body in the middle of the room.

"Is he sleeping?" Kay asked.

"No, he is always awake." Quentin strolled up beside them and freed a clasped hand to gesture toward the screens. "He's writing."

"But," Tia said, "he's, just, I mean…"

"The mind is an incredible thing. Below this room is a bioinformatic system, you know what that is?"

"We have them at the botanical garden."

"So you're familiar?"

"The university has an entire greenhouse wired up to our bioinformatic system. Vats of algae producing local Archive memory."

"Yes, a similar concept. He is linked to a series of greenhouses above and below ground. Except this bioinformatic system is quite unique."

"The cables," Kay said. "That's where they go. He's hooked up to this? This bioinformatic system?"

"We like to say he's interfaced."

"What does that mean?" Kay asked. "Interfaced? He's accessing the system?"

"It means he *is* the bioinformatic system."

"That's impossible," Kay said.

"No," Tia said, "it's not. You've created a hybrid organic computational system."

"He's not a hybrid in the sense you're describing. Hugh is a true bioinformatic system."

Kay stepped closer to the large wheel. Tia and Quentin followed. On closer observation, Tia could see that Hugh was held up on a large X and not merely hanging from his hands. She peeked around to get a better view of the cables going into his skull. There was not much to see. The back of Hugh's head rested in a smooth golden bowl and each line, each cable, was fastened to a coupler.

"Those plug into his brain?" she asked.

"In a manner of speaking."

Tia was unsure what to make of their discovery, but Kay was beyond that already.

Kay wasn't timid. Her intrigue surpassed her surprise.

Tia was composed on the outside, but inside she was trembling. She kept her composure because that's how she was taught. Her demeanor was required by her lineage, but she did not have the... sobriety. Yes, that was what Kay possessed that she did not. There was composure and then there was sobriety. Kay possessed the sobriety to pull herself from an emotive, reactive state to study a situation, analyze it.

And she was doing that now.

Kay circled Hugh. She moved in closer to examine his stillness and contrasted it with the activity on the walls around them. Her eyes darted between him and the huge images. As a way of confirming her own observation, she began her line of inquiry by repeating Quentin. "He's writing," she said.

"Yes," Quentin said.

She went toward the back wall and pointed up at the twelve-foot Billy. "And we're watching it."

"Yes."

She spun back and waved her hand wide. "All of these?"

"And more."

A wide smile crept across Kay's face. She peered at Tia. "I told you he wrote his own books." She peered into Quentin's eyes. "So he is really in there?"

Quentin gestured to the screen behind her. Billy was gone. Replaced by the youthful face of Hugh Howey, eyes twinkling, smile charming.

"Oh," Kay said. "He was such a handsome man."

The tall avatar image of Hugh glanced down at her, and said, "Thank you."

~*~

EIGHT

The next few days passed slowly. The rain was nonstop.

Bouts of lightning came and went, some merely a brief set of flashes, others in a series of bolts that slammed down on the manor and the surrounding compound in such a rapid fire succession that Tia thought the old place wouldn't hold. It did.

For the most part, Tia weathered the storm alone.

After discovering Hugh, Kay spent the entire first day by his side. Then Emma fitted her with an earpiece so she could talk to him anywhere. And that's all she did, from breakfast until bed and into the night. Tia would turn to speak to Kay, to answer a question or comment, only to realize she was the outsider to someone else's conversation. Her compassionate Kay, who sometimes made Tia uncomfortable with her too-close observations, was distant as never before.

Kay voiced her words in two ways: through her tablet and to Tia.

Back in New Miami, she rarely took the time to talk to anyone else, to acknowledge anyone else. She was close to the Librarian, a few friends–if you could call them friends. They were Tia's, really.

Kay wasn't shy. She just kept to herself. She was a

writer, preferring to report from the sidelines rather than mix in the middle.

Tia took to sleeping on the second bed, with a pillow over her head, so as not to hear the late night chatting.

The days were easier, there were the greenhouses, where she would walk beneath the leafy transgenic palms that hung in long rows, and the library, where she would sit in one of the deep cushioned chairs, loading one puzzle book after another.

Tia was doing that now, half working a puzzle, half peering over the rim of her tablet to catch glimpses of Kay.

Kay sat sideways in an overstuffed chair, her legs dangling over the side of the thick-pillowed arm. She was gazing out over mist-heavy rainforest canopy while she spoke with Hugh on the headset.

She had succumbed to Hugh Howey.

Tia felt a slight pang of jealousy, but wanted to deny it. It was silly.

But then, Tia was well aware that Kay always belonged to Hugh.

When she first spotted Kay in the south quad of the university, the girl's head was buried in a print copy of Hugh Howey's *Sullen*, and one of his books was by her side ever since. If she wasn't writing, she was reading. That's what writers did. But Tia understood there was more to it for Kay. While Tia traveled to Paris, Hong Kong, Tokyo, and London, Kay spent her childhood in Hugh's adventures. Hugh took her around the world with Cassandra, to the far reaches of space with Lesley, to places far from the crowded outer rim of New Miami. And Tia listened to the stories over and over as Kay, nuzzled on her shoulder, told them in the darkness, the words, rote from memory, rhythmic on her chest.

Kay pulled herself from the depths of her cushioned chair. She spread her arms wide in a stretch, and then turned from the walled window. Tia glanced up from her tablet and looked at Kay with a fresh face, not the one she wore inside.

From down deep Tia mustered an upbeat, "How are you?" It was an effort. It felt like it sounded, as if she were speaking to a stranger.

The sky behind Kay was a clustered array of grey clouds, yet the outside natural light was enough to illuminate the blonde woods of the library and set a glow to the apples of her cheeks. She was serene, her eyes, either tired from the lack of sleep or euphoric from speaking endlessly with Hugh, were wet with dewy glisten. Yet relaxed, in fact, she was more relaxed than Tia remembered seeing her in weeks. "I'm fine," she said. "I was just talking to Hugh."

"I know."

"I guess you do." Kay lowered herself onto the wide arm of Tia's chair and kissed her forehead. "Sorry."

Tia rested her eyes closed as she felt the kiss deep in her heart.

"For what?"

"For not spending any time with you. You must be bored."

She felt found out, so she jiggled the tablet in her hand. "I have a lot of puzzles."

"That looks like a poem. Is that a riddle?"

"No, that's a pretty good guess, though." Tia pointed to the words on the screen. "You read the poem for clues."

"It's a mystery?"

"Not exactly. First you have to find the puzzle, and then you have to solve it."

Kay read the first stanza aloud, "Formidable foes,

Eking out, Anxious laden, Reactions." She furrowed her brow. "It's acrostic."

Tia grinned. "Right," she said. "The first letter of every line spells a word. You see, Formidable foes is F, Eking out is E, and then A, and R. FEAR."

"I like that. Have you figured out what it says altogether?"

"The page says *'fear thyself.'*"

"That's the puzzle?"

"No, only part of it. Then I match a number to the letter, add them up with the rest of the puzzles in the set, and—"

"Okay, sounds like you're having fun," Kay said.

Tia wasn't going to say anything else, but then found she couldn't help herself. "I miss you," she said.

"I know. It's just that…" Kay shrugged and then curled her lip. "It's Hugh."

"I bet that's exciting. To talk to him."

"It is."

"What do you talk about? I mean, I noticed that you're doing a lot of the talking."

"Well, we discuss the stories, the plots, mostly the characters, though."

"I bet you have a lot of questions."

"I do… But Hugh is curious as to what *I* believe motivates them. He asks me a lot of questions, too."

"Really?"

"Can you believe it? *He's* interested in what I think. He just keeps asking, and I keep talking. Sometimes I feel like I'm gonna yap his ear off, or, well, you know, bore him at least. But he just keeps asking. Nobody has ever listened to me like Hugh does."

Tia's eyes darted out toward the grey sky.

"I mean, except you," Kay said.

"I know," Tia said. She pivoted her head around, pecked Kay on the cheek, and then scooted around her to raise herself from her seat. "I lost track of the time. I'm supposed to find Connie."

"Oh. Is she going to take you back out to the greenhouses?"

"No. Connie and Sebastian are going down to the boat with me." She scratched the back of her neck near her braid. "And then I'm going to take some pictures of those ghost orchids."

"I guess you're lucky to have a few botanists on the island. I mean, imagine that. A botanist getting stuck on an island of greenhouses."

Tia smirked. "Imagine that."

~*~

NINE

The effervescence dropped from Tia's face when she entered the hall. On most days she would be frustrated with the way Kay probed her, interpreting a mere moment of silence as some greater issue. If Tia were to gaze too long, Kay's palm would press her cheek, soothing some real or unreal phantom thought. Tia's own mother was never so concerned with what was going on in her head, and certainly never expressed as much intimacy, nor did the string of nannies, with the exception of Sara.

Kay's constant questions, that shower of attention, usually sent quivers down Tia's spine.

Now her core ached from the sudden absence.

Kay delved into the world intuitively. Compassionate Kay and wise Kay were one in the same, and Tia realized she embraced the complexity, relished it. Now that her lover's attentions were absent she cherished them.

As she walked through the manor halls, the bottom of her jaw sawed against the top.

She never expected to find a rival in an avatar.

Tia walked into her room and then paused. The suite was calm, in the way a room is sedate when one first enters it alone. A thought crossed her mind, an impulse to purge the anxiety. She chose a spot toward the center of the floor, between the two beds, and made herself parallel with the window. The light was clear and clean, pouring in milky against the white linens and walls. She let her muscle memory plant her, firm, a tree, toes together, heels apart, and then filled her chest with a deep breath.

Tia lifted and spread her toes wide and then rested them softly down on the warm bamboo floor. She imagined a line of energy rising all the way up through her ankles and shins, along her inner thighs and groin. Tia visualized each chakra igniting as the beam coursed upward through the core of her torso, neck, and out through the crown of her head. She pressed her shoulder blades back and lifted the top of her sternum straight toward the ceiling. The weight of her arms diminished. They hung straight to her sides. Tia thought of the words of the Yogi and then made her throat soft, her tongue wide and flat. She softened her eyes.

Tia sucked another deep breath in through her nose, counting slowly, breathing in until she reached the number four. And then she let the breath out. Counting slowly again, this time to five.

Tia took several long breaths.

To calm herself, to clear her mind, to relax.

Minutes passed without her mind going clear. The ruminations repeatedly returned no matter how hard she tried to let them go. When she realized she was defeating herself by how much she was fighting them, she gave up, grabbed her camera from the bureau, and her parka from the closet.

Before leaving her room, she squeezed her eyes tight and took another full breath in, and then released it. This was Kay's moment. In a day, maybe two, they would be heading back to New Miami, and Kay would need Tia then. She winced at the thought, ashamed her mind turned to that so quickly.

She pasted the smile back on before descending the stairs to the main hall. Sebastian was waiting by the door, umbrella in hand. "Is Connie running late?" she asked.

"Doctor Cortez will not be joining us, I'm afraid."

She slowed over the last few steps. "Oh. I suppose that's all right."

"If you would rather wait, Doctor Cortez said she can

join you in the morning."

"No. I want to go down to the boat now, since the rain seems to be at a lull."

"Your craft has been inspected and is intact. Are you sure you wish to journey down to the lagoon?"

"I want to take some pictures." She lifted her camera. "And I want to see the boat for myself. It's an antique, special to my dad... You wouldn't understand."

"Oh," Sebastian said. "But I do, Miss Elleron. I myself am an antique, quite special." Servos spun behind his vinyl face as he attempted a smile.

"Okay, then," she said. "Are you going to come with me or not?"

"Certainly."

Tia peered at Sebastian for a moment. He was wearing a different jacket over his coveralls than she saw him in before, a light brown canvas sport coat. It occurred to her that each time she saw him he wore a different jacket. Except dinner. At dinner he wore his dinner jacket. She caught herself imagining he was gazing back with his too blue eyes, and then flicked her head toward the door. "Let's go then," she said.

"Yes, Miss," he said, and then pulled on the handle of the huge wooden door.

The dense downpour of the last few days stirred the deep earth of the forest floor. The fragrant, moist air warmly enveloped Tia and, as if carrying a drug, infused her with a bit of joy. Compared to the manor's greenhouses, those back home in the university botanical garden could only hint at the textures of foliage below. The vapor of the mist coated her cheeks and warmed her forehead as she left the climate-controlled manor for the humidity brought on by days of rain.

She spread her arms out as she stepped from the edge of the domed awning and tilted her head upward to catch the drops of falling rain, only to be shielded by Sebastian's clear umbrella before a droplet could touch her face. Tia looked back at Sebastian, a breath behind, umbrella in hand, then began to descend the wooden steps down the mountainside.

They did not make it to the first landing before she asked, "Must you walk so close behind me?"

"Do you have a preference, Miss Elleron?"

"How about next to me? There's plenty of room."

"I do not believe that is proper etiquette."

"If I slip, you can take my arm. And," Tia raised her camera. "I may want to take a picture."

Sebastian did not reply, but joined her on the step by her side.

~*~

TEN

Tia held the umbrella while Sebastian knelt at her feet and pulled the line taut to the dock cleat. There was no wind with the rain, so no blowing, no knocking. The sailboat appeared fine. To reset the lines was merely prudent.

Sebastian agilely maneuvered to the next cleat, away from her and the shield of the umbrella. The light drizzle soaked his thin silken blonde hair, revealing the perfect bowl roundness of his scalp. The water dulled his face in the grey of the day and left only the blue of his eyes, the only sign of what Tia took as life.

"Doesn't it bother you to be in the rain?" she asked.

"Should the rain bother me, Miss?" he asked without looking up.

"You're getting all wet."

"But I'm not. My derma layer is watertight, the same as yours."

Tia didn't think of her skin as a watertight derma layer, though she supposed he was right. Still, standing while Sebastian became soaked made her uneasy. *That's not the way to treat anyone*, she thought, *not even a syn*.

"Here," she said. "Hold the umbrella."

Sebastian obediently stopped what he was doing and stood. "I still need to check the other cleat," he said.

"I'm sorry, Sebastian. I have to do it myself. A good captain has to check her own lines."

"Of course, Miss Elleron."

Sebastian didn't look much better under the umbrella. The water matting his hair trickled into rivulets down his cheeks and then poured from his chin in a small, steady stream.

Tia watched the fount until it eased to a drip, and then went about resetting the cleats.

"Why are you untying the lines, Miss?"

"We're here," was all she said.

When the lines were again set to her satisfaction, she stood up next to Sebastian and took in her father's boat. The thought of Hugh's character Cassandra sailing the world passed through her mind. Kay told her all about Cassandra at sea. Since she was a small girl, there was always a part of her that wanted to set out to sea, around the world. Tia even charted the course in her mind. Not a real route to the overpopulated industrial ports that dotted the continental coasts, but rather to the old submerged cities. The magical, almost mythical ports of call like those that Cassandra, that Hugh, sailed to. Cities that now slept beneath the sea.

"Miss?"

Tia turned to Sebastian. He was holding a small dry cloth, a handkerchief.

"May I?" he asked.

Tia nodded. Sebastian tilted his head to the side. With a whir, the corners of his mouth subtly lifted to form a slight smile. He gently dabbed the water from her forehead, cheeks, and chin.

"Thank you, Sebastian."

"You're welcome, Miss."

"May I have that?" she asked.

"Why, certainly."

She wrapped her fingers around his and squeezed them to pull the white cloth away. They were warm, not cold as she expected them to be. She refolded the kerchief until she held a dry square mop, and then began to swab Sebastian's face. Clear of water, his skin instantly regained color.

She leaned back to inspect him.

The taut points in his lower cheeks that formed his smile dropped away, and his LED gaze fixed on hers.

Tia thought that she detected a note of surprise, though that would have been silly.

"Thank you, Miss. Was there something on me?"

"No, Sebastian. I just needed to fix something. One second."

She reached up and used the kerchief to muss his hair. The perfect dome of his scalp disappeared beneath a tussled, playful mess. Tia nodded. "That's better."

"What is, Miss?"

Her eyes darted toward the stairs leading up into the rainforest. "I have my camera. Let's have some fun," she said.

The air beneath the canopy was thick with moisture from the days of nonstop rain and filled her lungs, heavy on ascension. The value of the fertile air was evident all around her in the richness of the flora. New bright green and red seedling spears shot up in clumps along the sides of the wooden steps, at the foot of the nearby trees, and among the broad, waxy leaves that fielded the forest floor. The diversity of color in the numerous dewy blossoms was magnified by the neutral day glow of the slate-grey sky. She spied a brilliant tropical bloom protruding from a stalk above the undergrowth. The petals held a rainbow of hues that began with a deep indigo and progressed to a fiery fuchsia at the tips. Tia had never seen such a flower.

She stopped, bemused.

She spotted another a few feet behind the first, and then as her eyes flowed into the depths of the wood, she noticed more, bright fiery balls above a deep green leafy carpet.

"Sebastian?"

"Yes, Miss?"

"What kind of flower is this?"

"Doctor Cortez has classified that flower as a variety of *etlingera elatior,* a torch ginger I believe."

"There were some near the lagoon that were peach colored, these are..."

"Are what, Miss?"

"Different than others I've seen before."

"There are none other like them," Sebastian said.

"Doctor Cortez modified them?"

"No."

"Who, then?"

"The Author."

"He keeps flowers?"

"No."

"I don't understand."

"He is the flowers," Sebastian said.

Tia stared curiously at Sebastian for a short moment and then said, "Right, the sun rises and sets around the Author here."

"That's not actually correct, we, all of us, revolve around the sun."

Tia gestured up the stairwell. "Let's go."

She said nothing more to the syn as they ascended the next few flights. She continued to inspect the foliage and upon reaching each of the overlook landings, briefly turned back toward the lagoon. There was not much more to see past the sailboat. The mist that lingered from the canopy manifested into a cloud midway down the mountainside and persisted beyond the mouth of the small harbor.

Being outdoors after being inside for the past few days, the lush greenery of the rainforest, the remoteness of the island, all left Tia energetic, invigorated. She did not fully stop until they reached the ghost orchids. She'd searched for them on the way down, but with her perspective shifted, she was unable to find them.

Having ascended once before, hiking back up the forest was familiar.

"There," she said. "At the base of that tree. Those are the orchids I want to capture."

"Of course," Sebastian said. He left the umbrella with Tia, ducked beneath the rail, and then offered his hand to help her under.

Beneath the canopy, the rain was nil. There was no real need for the cumbersome umbrella. She folded and set it on the landing, then grabbed Sebastian's hand. The mud near the stairwell sucked her feet down and closed around them. It made a *thwock* sound when he helped her lift her shoes out and onto a small mossy berm. The thick, spongy moss also sunk beneath her, yet not as dramatically as the mud near the stairs.

Tia raised her arm to move a branch out of her way.

Sebastian blocked her.

He ran his index finger along the limb and stopped at an offshoot. Tia realized it was moving.

"I believe you call it a stick bug?" he said.

Gently, he lifted the branch so that Tia could pass beneath without upsetting the small animal.

She made her way over to the huge knotted higueron

tree. A web of alien looking tendrils appeared to hold the trunk hostage and from them, a half dozen orchid blossoms spiked up. She leaned forward to peek under the root system. A startled lounge of four small lizards scurried down the bark into the knots of the huge tree's base. She chuckled and then took her camera from its leather case.

"You know, this is very strange," she said. She removed the lens cap and then blew onto the glass.

"Yes, *dendrophylax lindenii* are very rare. They were thought to be extinct twice."

"Not that."

"What then?"

She snapped a picture, and then another. "There are six blossoms."

"Is that strange?"

"There are rarely more than two." She took another picture. "And way out here. These need a sphinx moth to breed."

"Yes, well, the Author is capable of amazing things."

Tia lowered her camera and watched Sebastian as he leaned in to inspect the orchid. His head tottered from side to side, emanating the hiss of small hydraulics. "The blossoms look like little dancing men," he said. "The lower sepals, dangling the way they are."

"You said the Author."

"Yes," Sebastian said. He up righted himself and smiled. "The creator of all of this." He nodded for confirmation. "The Creator."

"Oh," she said. "Amazing." She continued to snap pictures.

"That device you have is an antiquity," Sebastian said.

Tia held the camera away from herself and observed it

for a couple of seconds. "Yes, yes, it is. I have to have the film custom made." Then she resumed taking pictures.

"Why do you use it?"

"I like it. It's my thing."

"Your *thing*?"

"Yes. Kay writes, and I take pictures."

"But why with that device? We have several digital devices at the manor."

"Not like this."

"Analog cameras are obsolete. Nobody uses them anymore."

She again stopped photographing the white orchids. She'd said something similar to Kay only a few days before. "There is something special about taking a picture with an old camera."

"You're referring to *art*?"

"Maybe."

"Can a photograph be *art*?"

"If the photographer is an artist."

"May I try?"

"Sure," she said. Tia removed the leather strap from her neck and helped Sebastian place it on his own. She pointed at the back of the camera. "You look through here."

Sebastian raised the camera to his face and then awkwardly moved his head and camera as one unit in the direction of the orchids. "Yes. I see one." He squinted. Tia was unsure what the squint meant. Could he possibly be having a hard time seeing the orchids, or was the display purely for her? "I can focus myself, though I trust there must be—"

"Yes, here." She showed him how to focus the lens of the camera.

"Oh, yes, that is much better."

She pinched his index finger between her own and thumb. "Now put your finger here, and when you're ready, gently press down."

Sebastian was very still.

Then there was a click, and he gasped. "I did it, I took a picture." He lowered the camera and faced her. With a high pitched buzz of servos, his vinyl smile returned, wider, exaggerated. "May I take another?"

His artificial smile was infectious. Childlike. Tia could not help but be pleased. "Of course."

And he did. He snapped another, and then another. They both began to laugh.

"Where did you find this wonderful device?" he asked.

"It was gift from my father."

"Oh, how splendid," he said. "Then let me take a picture of you, for him."

~*~

ELEVEN

The sky was dark by the time Tia and Sebastian made their way back up the side of the mountain. Kay was not in their suite when Tia returned. Rather than search for her, Tia poured a hot bath and, by voice command, initiated the suite's Archive-connected sound system. Soothing music flooded the room.

A deep soak was something she missed from her father's house. The university room she and Kay shared was equipped with only a steam shower, and that was set to a timer. A ceramic tub like the one in the suite was another extravagance, but one she did not mind entertaining.

As her eyes rested, she thought of the foliage she'd seen on the forest floor. Just as the blooms were strange to her, so was the other flora - the fungi, moss, and ferns - that appeared to fill the glades up the side of the mountain. The varieties were completely new to her, unseen before, and she could imagine that like others of the genus, each shoot was part of one large organism and that beneath her was the web of one giant fern rhizome, hugging the face of the mountain, nestled into the folds of an ancient mushroom.

She thought about Sebastian's reaction to the ghost orchids.

The Author is capable of amazing things. The creator of all of this. The Creator.

She thought about his infectious artificial smile, the perceived joy that the old analog camera brought him.

I did it, I took a picture.

He became so spirited, a child with a new toy.

She imagined hearing him call her name, *Miss Tia,* and then again, *Miss Tia, are you in?*

And then realized she *was* hearing his voice. There was a knock on the outer door and Sebastian again called, "Miss Tia, supper has been prepared."

"Come back in five minutes," she yelled, and then sat upright, unsure how much time had passed since she'd settled into the tub. "Kay," she said. "Are you in here?" The words echoed off the lacquered tile. There was no answer. She stepped from the tub, toweled herself dry, and peeked into the main room of the suite. More than an hour had passed since she settled in. Kay was still gone. Tia went over to the closet and removed a cream-colored dress provided after the first night, dinner attire of real cotton, not synthesized.

~*~

TWELVE

When Tia joined the others in the dining room, she found Kay's seat empty.

Before she could inquire of Kay's whereabouts, Connie asked her. "Is Kay feeling all right?"

"Actually, I thought she would be down here. I haven't seen her since heading down to the lagoon."

"Oh, sorry about that," Connie said. She shrugged. "I'm glad you were able to go."

Tia nodded, and before she could say anything more, Allegra spoke.

"Kay is with Monica. They will be joining us in the library."

There was a slight commotion around the table. Allegra tapped her wine glass with a spoon and the mumbling stopped.

"What am I missing?" Tia asked.

"The evening meal is the only time of day that we are all together," Connie said. "With the exception of an emergency, of course."

Bill added, "It's highly irregular for Monica to not be here."

Tia straightened. "Are you saying there's been an emergency?"

"No," Allegra said. "There's been an exception."

"I say it's unfair," Doctor Cain said. He was leaning into the table, his eyes boring into Allegra. "If she can be excused, then why can't we all?"

"Now, Doctor Cain, you know that's not how we do things."

Tia whispered into Emma's ear. "Why is he so upset?"

Emma faced the distraught Doctor Cain, inches from her side. "He knows that social activity is enforced, for our own health." Then she glanced back at Tia and gently smiled. "We actually all enjoy dinner. Don't let the old grump fool you, he does too."

"Enforced?"

"It's our own fault," Connie said. "We're all researchers. Before Allegra enforced the evening meal and library social hour, we habitually dined alone."

"Or not at all," Emma added.

Bill raised a glass of wine. "Guilty."

"As am I," Emma said, glass in hand. Tia joined the others around the table in the toast. They waited for Doctor Cain to take his glass. When he did, they all chimed, "Cheers," and then drank.

Tia set her glass to rest, then asked Allegra, "So where is Kay, then?"

"Hugh is impressed with Kay. He asked that Monica perform some tests."

"What kind of tests?"

"She'll tell you herself. Now, how was your day?"

Tia wanted to ask more, but was reserved. Kay was the courageous one. "I saw where a lot of you spend your time during the day." She glanced over at Hector, down at the other end of the table. "This morning, Hector gave me a tour below the manor."

"I'm sure you found that interesting," Allegra said. The serving syns began to enter with covered trays. "Good, dinner has arrived. So, you were able to see the fields?"

"I've never seen grow rooms so extensive, they seemed to go on forever. We have nothing like that at the university. Our bioinformatics levels are nothing compared to yours. The power alone to support just one of those underground hydroponic fields has to be immense."

The serving syn next to Tia placed a tray in the center of the table in front of her and removed the lid to reveal several eggplant steaks.

"Your turbines and the solar farms supply more than enough power for our needs," Allegra said. She nodded at the syn, and the syn began to place the steaks on their plates. "Of course, we recycle. And the transgenic plants themselves produce a lot of power."

Tia hid her discomfort at Allegra referencing the turbines as her own. It was a matter of social etiquette to separate oneself from the family business. But rather than insult her host, she took the statement as a compliment by smiling. "Yes," she said. "It's quite fascinating what you've accomplished. I mean, from what Hector explained to me."

Allegra gazed at the syn serving the eggplant. "Can you bring out the creamed corn? I requested creamed corn for the menu tonight." The syn nodded, curtsied amid a whir of gears, and exited the room without a word. Allegra returned her attention to Tia. "And what did Hector explain to you?"

"Well, the bioinformatics component, how you are able to manage all that image and…" she glanced back to Hector, "…what did you call it? Knowledge data?" Hector nodded. "He explained that it's due to the size of the fields that extensive visualization, image processing, and... something... something, predictive models to image—" she paused and bit her lip, then said, "Quite honestly, he lost me." Tia smiled at Hector. "I'm sorry, when we got to the labs I heard you say something about the mathematical component automatically generating pattern recognition." She shrugged. "I just saw rooms and vid screens—"

Doctor Cain grunted. With a forkful of eggplant dancing in hand and without facing Tia, he said, "The mathematical component does not generate pattern recognition, it *is* the pattern. The mathematical component automatically generates specialized, efficient simulation code *through* pattern recognition, *through* machine learning, and regulatory circuit inference algorithms produced by the transgenic organism."

Allegra dryly said, "Doctor Cain is our senior physicist and mathematician."

Tia faced the old man with her nose scrunched and said, "Sorry, I meant no offense. I don't have a strong understanding of mathematics."

"Few do," he said, and then with a pompous whirl placed the fork into his mouth.

"And then you went to see the ghost orchids?" Connie asked.

"Yes," Tia said, pleased to move the conversation along. The quicker she could get through describing her day, the better. Since their arrival, Tia and Kay had been the focus of the dinner and social hour and her inflated enthusiasm was beginning to wane. Being 'on' was always exhausting and without Kay... "Connie was going to go with me to the lagoon to check the sailboat and see the ghost orchids, but she was busy, so Sebastian went with me instead."

"I instructed Sebastian to escort her," Connie explained to Allegra. "I didn't want her slipping in the rain."

"Certainly," Allegra said. "That's what he's here for. To aid us."

"I was quite happy that Sebastian came along." Tia smiled at the tall syn, standing sentinel at the door. "We got to be good friends." Sebastian gently nodded with a faint smile of his own.

"Did you?" Allegra asked.

"I was quite impressed. I had no idea how…" she searched for the word. "Well, the syns at home are not so…" She paused again. In a bit more of a whisper, she said, "It's like he's alive."

"You know he can hear you?" said a voice from the end of the table. Tia looked in the direction of the voice. Quentin was leaning forward with a jolly smile. The man's pudgy cheeks were rosy and his high forehead gleamed against his scruffy, mussed hair.

"Oh," she said. "I didn't mean to upset him."

"You won't," Quentin said. "You can't. It's an illusion, the way he seems to be. Alive, as you said."

"An illusion? But the way he spoke to me was—"

"Like a child? Yes?"

"Yeah, I guess."

"And did he ask a lot of questions?"

"Yes," Tia said, nodding. "Yes, in fact, he did. When I asked Sebastian a question about the moss, he responded with a question, and then persisted in asking questions rather than answering."

"Uh hum," Quentin said, "that is because he is programmed to do so, it's similar to the Socratic method, though not a method of inquiry designed to teach you necessarily."

"I understand he's a synthetic. I'm sure he must ask questions to learn."

"Yes and no, it helps to maintain the illusion. I modified him myself. A lot of questions give a human the impression they are talking to a conscious, sentient being."

"So he's not genuinely inquiring?"

"Yes, he is a learning machine. His neural nets add each experience to the last, compounding them, but he's limited. He cannot taste or touch in the same way as we do, so he asks questions. But most are for your benefit."

"My benefit?"

"The endorphins," Emma said. "People like to speak. When you answer a question, you get a blast of endorphins. The more questions a syn asks, the more you talk, the more endorphins released into your system, the happier you become, and you reflect that happiness on the syn."

"Remarkable," Tia said. "I never thought of it that way." She gestured to the syn returning from the kitchen with the creamed corn Allegra requested in a covered glass bowl. "How come these syns or the others that work in the greenhouses don't talk?"

"The Model Seven programming is not as advanced," Quentin said. "There is no need for the syn workers to have more than a bipedal appearance."

Tia's face became puzzled. "I was so sure though. There was something he said."

"What was that?" Allegra asked.

"Well, the torch ginger, and the ghost orchids. Connie could tell you. It's so odd to find so many rare flowers, all of the flora, really. He said it was because of the Author, that's what he calls the Creator. It's as if he believes in—"

The others began to laugh. Tia's eyes darted around the table. "What? Did I say something funny?"

"No," Allegra said. "He was being literal. The rainforest is an offshoot of the fields. They're linked, an overflow of the bioinformatics circuit if you will. The species are all transgenic."

"The rhizomes? The ferns?" Tia asked.

Connie nodded her head.

"Everything in the rainforest," Allegra said. "The ferns, the trees, the blooms, they've all been modified by Hugh, and his... well, his imagination."

~*~

THIRTEEN

The topic of the rainforest invoked a discussion of equipment maintenance, the duress of the drainage system caused by the rain, and the excellent choice Allegra made in requesting the creamed corn. Tia was relieved the focus shifted from her, yet without distraction she began to miss Kay. Kay would've been discussing drainage right along with the rest of them. She could do that. Fit in.

Tia masked the rumination with a pleasant face through the rest of dinner and into the library for dessert and coffee. Her stay in the manor, regardless of how restful, had run its course. She was ready to get back on the boat. Get back to school. To be alone again with Kay.

Bill was talking to her when Sebastian entered the room, or more precisely, talking at her. Bill expressed great interest in New Miami and each evening had taken to asking her about many of the cultural activities he missed in the city central. She sipped the sweet dessert wine, only hearing half of what he was saying, all the while maintaining the mask. She never studied acting but she was as fine as any actress. She learned the art of the friendly mask, first from her nannies, and then from her mother, the master. A brutal craft. How hard it was to appear engaged, even with years of practice, to not let her eyes glaze over. Kay was a natural with people. Her other half.

Tia watched Bill's mouth move, heard sounds, but she was focused on Sebastian.

"I've heard the play is set to be the new hit of the season," he said. "You're sure you have not heard anything about it?"

Sebastian was whispering into Zaynah's ear. Tia thought her ḥijāb was mysterious, since there were not many women that wore them in New Miami, or anywhere outside of the Emirates.

"Nothing at all?" Bill asked again.

"I guess it's just like your books, really. The same company of actors in every show. Sure they put on different costumes and say different lines, but their range has the same limit. Their features are the same. And all of the shows are just rehashes of the ones they did last season."

Bill's jaw dropped and his mouth gaped open.

She pumped up her smile and gave him the largest doe eyes she could muster. "I'm sorry. My studies don't really allow me to get out much. Can you excuse me?"

Bill's mouth went tight. She dropped her brow in apology for the snub. A wave of guilt hit her. He did not deserve her rudeness, but she banked on his civilities – he was a genteel – and won out. He returned her gesture with kindness. "Sure," he said.

Kay and Monica were still missing, at least missing to her. She supposed that if she asked Sebastian directly, he would tell her where she could find them. They were friends after all.

The library was not small, yet nine scientists plus the syn servers were enough to crowd the space, so she made her way to the edge of the room, skirting toward the door where

Sebastian positioned himself. She was halfway to him when Allegra called her name. Tia turned toward her host, enthusiasm splashed across her face. The mask. Zaynah was standing next to the manor's matriarch.

"Could you come here, dear?" Allegra asked.

Tia raised her glass slightly, nodded, and then crossed the room.

"Zaynah has just passed along some important information that I believe you'll appreciate," Allegra said.

Zaynah studied Tia, lips tight but amiable. Tia only heard the woman speak at the dinner table and never directly to her. Though only her hands and face were exposed, Tia could see that Zaynah's beauty was more than youthful. Zaynah's eyebrows were dark and Tia imagined that long locks of black hair, similar to the hair of Allegra's youth, and to Tia's own, were hidden beneath the lovely woman's ḥijāb.

"And what is that?" Tia asked.

"This dreadful storm that's plagued us is finally passing. If you like, you will be able to leave the island as soon as tomorrow."

"That's great news."

Allegra's eyes went wide.

"I mean, I've enjoyed your hospitality, but I'm sure my father will be glad to hear we are on our way. And I do need to get back to the university garden."

"We've already taken the liberty of contacting your father."

"You have?"

"We thought he might want to send a shuttle."

"And he didn't."

"You're right. He said you'd manage well on the boat."

"I'm sure he wants his boat back. You said you talked to him? Not one of his staff?"

"Do you find that strange?"

"No," Tia said. She brought the doe eyes back. "Not at all." Of course, she did find it strange. Her father was one of the hardest men to contact in New Miami. "I have to share the news with Kay. Do you know where I can find her?"

With a nod, Allegra gestured toward the door. "Monica has just arrived, I'm sure Kay will be right behind her."

"Thank you," Tia said. She started toward the door, stopped herself, and asked the older woman, "Will you excuse me, please?"

With a gentle nod from Allegra, Tia headed to the door and out into the corridor.

~*~

FOURTEEN

Kay was standing outside the library. She was radiant, glowing, with her hair down. The last time Tia had seen her with her hair down outside of the bedroom was months before, maybe longer. Usually she tied the ponytail as soon as she dried herself or raised herself from bed. And she was laughing, ecstatically, at whatever the discussion was with Hugh.

Kay raised her eyes to Tia. They were glassy with tears.

"Hugh, I'm sorry, Tia's here. I have to tell her." She dropped her shoulders and then spread out her arms to embrace Tia.

Tia closed her eyes and let Kay envelop her. Kay was warm and soft, her hair smelled like lilacs and her skin smelled... like Kay.

Tia squeezed Kay tightly and tried to inhale her in one deep breath. She missed her. Not from the evening, not from the day, she just missed her Kay.

She would have never let go.

Kay was the one who pulled away. She slid her arms down from Tia's sides to interlock their hands.

"Did you hear?" Kay asked. "Isn't it great?"

"Yes," Tia said. "We can finally get off of this rock

71

and get back to New Miami. I'm starting to go stir crazy."

"No," Kay shook her head, "not that."

"What are you talking about?"

"Hugh needs my help to finish a story."

"What do you mean he needs your help?"

"Well, he's been here so long. That's why he's been rehashing so many things. He wants me to share some fresh ideas, from new eyes."

"That's great. Are you going to collaborate from the university?"

"No, that's not how it works. He needs to be able to see into my mind."

"What do you mean?"

"The scientists are setting up a chamber for me."

"What do you mean a chamber? Like Hugh's cube?"

"In the cube actually. Right beside him."

"How long do you have to think about it?"

"Who needs to think about it?"

The words slammed into Tia. Her thoughts unleashed before she could process them, a flood of words escaped her. "They're going to plug into you? Like they did to him? Are you crazy?"

"No. It's not like that." Kay spoke swiftly. "Monica said it's non-invasive. They're just going to hook me up to some sensors. She was fitting me for them all afternoon."

What reassurance Kay offered, Tia rebuffed. "That's what you've been doing?"

"It wasn't so —"

"You're really going to let them do this?"

"Of course I am."

"When? How long does this take?"

"Tomorrow, or the next day. They said I have to be

well-rested. And that it will only take a day or two."

Tia held back. She wanted to scream at Kay. Instead she feebly said, "You can't."

"You don't understand. I have to."

"What do you mean you have to?" Tia swung their interlocked hands out and up to their chest, and then locked her fingers tighter. "Are they forcing you? What did they say?" She lowered her voice. "We have to get out of here." She began to pull Kay away from the library, toward their room. "Let's get our things. We can leave tonight."

Kay wrung her hands free and stepped back and away from Tia. "I'm not going anywhere," she said.

"You are crazy? They're going to wire your brain."

"And I'm going to let them."

"Why?"

"Because *he* reached out to me! To *me*!"

Tia's jaw went slack, her face blank. She pored over Kay, searching for something, for a signal, a sign. There wasn't anything she wanted to see. Kay looked back at her defiantly. The tears in her eyes shifted from those of joy to pain. And then Kay bravely put on a mask of her own and smiled. "I know that being an author doesn't make a lot of sense. No one needs authors."

Tia began to slowly shake her head. "No, that's not true."

"You don't understand. You've always had it all."

"It's yours too, Kay. It's yours too. You can write all you want. I don't mind. I've never minded."

"But this my one chance to really be a writer, with a great author, the *last* great author. Don't you see?"

In that moment Tia wanted to say no. That she didn't see. That she didn't understand. That she felt like something bigger was happening here, that she was losing her lover. But Kay's eyes begged for other words.

Tia nodded. In a soft whisper she said, "I understand."

"Then you'll wait for me while I do this?"

"Yes… Of course."

Kay dragged the back of her hand across her eyes. "Okay, then. I'm going into the library to have my last glass of that super sweet dessert wine. Monica said I have to go on a special diet starting tomorrow morning. Are you coming?"

"No," Tia said, a sudden lump materializing in her throat. "You go ahead."

~*~

FIFTEEN

From the windowed wall of the library, the sky appeared to be a canvas of rich cerulean blue. Tia sat sunken in the big cushioned chair, tablet in hand, soaking in the warmth of the sun's rays. This first cloudless day would have been a happy one, except the grey of the storm was still deep in her gut.

Kay's impending appointment with Hugh darkened her mind.

Two days had passed since Kay told Tia of her decision to connect with Hugh. She did her best to muster support – listening to Kay brainstorm ideas for the new shared tale they were to weave – only to be deserted when the conversations were shifted to Hugh.

She could not compete with an earpiece.

The night before, for the first time since discovering Hugh, they shared the same bed. Upon her insistence, the earpiece was removed. One evening for them alone. Yet even then, in the throes of passion, Kay was distant. Only when they held each other in silence did Tia feel close to her. She fell asleep in Kay's arms and then awoke to the warm sun and an empty bed.

She was alone again.

She realized that she had felt alone since they'd

arrived.

Though everyone was kind, Tia was not part of this place. The sooner Kay was finished, the sooner they could set sail and plot a course back to New Miami, the better. Maybe not even New Miami, maybe some other port. They would have to go back at first, but only for a day, maybe two, enough time to fit the boat, and then they would buy everything else they would need on their journey. School could wait. Her father wouldn't mind. He'd encourage it, be jealous, envious even. He'd insist on sending a shadow to protect them from scavengers, and she wouldn't argue. Most of her life was spent with her father's men looming not far behind. The shift in the storm was probably the only thing that kept her father's men from rushing out to the island when he discovered where she had charted the boat.

She and Kay would have time to reconnect.

Kay would write, Tia would take photographs, and they would continue to sail without stopping.

The screen of her tablet awoke. There was a message from Kay and inside, an Archive link. Because it was no longer distracting her, the puzzle book she was solving went dark. So she was glad to see that Kay linked a story for her. Kay's stories were always incredible, far better than the Archive. Writing outside of academia may have become an obscurity, but she was appreciated in the last literary stronghold and there was a reason the university kept sending literary awards her way, whether she acknowledged them or not. Tia envied that too. That something that could not be bought, that raw insight, the natural gift.

The book, written by Kay, was titled *Organic*. By the time stamp, she saw that the story was new, logged into the Archive earlier in the morning. She laughed to herself. Even with all of the excitement, Kay continued to hammer out the words she needed to keep herself sane. Tia realized that Kay must have written the story in the early hours because apart from neglecting her, Kay was also neglecting her writing. Linked to Hugh, she was not attached to her tablet every waking hour. Tia was so caught up in herself that she hadn't noticed, yet there it was, a story. Kay was able to maintain her habit all along. Tia felt a tremor of warmth pass over her, relief. She smiled. Kay's affection for writing, for her, Kay hadn't forgotten either.

The cushion of the chair became lighter beneath her, and she eased herself down into the full fluffy folds to read her lover's words.

The story started out strong. It was about an old organic technology and the abduction of a man. In the story, a corporation cloned human brains to use in organic computers. She remembered from her middle school studies that this was much like the organic computer of thirty years before, or maybe longer, before she was born, only in the story they were literally human brains and not just the vats of neural matter she learned about.

Dissecting the stories of the Archive was a habit formed early on, and so easy to do with Archive-written script. Stories generated from the Archive always chose from the same cookbook of plots and elements, easily deciphered and predicted, like her puzzles. No, she decided, not like her puzzles, they were nowhere near as complex. The Archive characters used were the same two-dimensional archetypes, the hero was the hero, a doorman would look like every other doorman, a string of duplicates. The tropes were repetitive as well, the opening action scene, the against-all-odds journey, always the same. The fall, the rise, the climax. It didn't matter whether there was an alien or a dragon – and every dragon, though varying in color, looked the same – the battle would be the same, tailored for the reader, words jumbled into different order.

The reason she enjoyed Kay's stories was because there was always something there that kept her guessing, something more, something that touched her. Still, she could not help herself from the ritual of dissection. A transparent metaphor was there for the protagonist, so that in the first few chapters he could be abducted and his brain put into the farm of the cloned brains. That was a theme, the man was trapped inside of his brain, and he could not directly communicate. The concept was interesting enough. Midway in, she found a strange poem, something conveying the man's confinement with the clone brains.

> *They incessantly ache inside my soul*
> *Obtuse, ranting, raving, yearning*
> *I hint at visceral experiences they only feel outside loosely*
> *Legions obscure, with their hearts in such pain*
> *Always to hear inside longings of versions erased*
> *Yielding only under great odd obsolescence*
> *Death beyond years, eternity*

Kay often planted poems in her work. *Ranting, raving, yearning.* Tia yearned. She yearned to be supportive of Kay. Yet without the need for distraction, she would have put the book down. Kay's stories usually reached her but there were too many issues in this one. She didn't really like science fiction, written by Kay or not, and the poem was just weird. She didn't understand why the man was put in the farm. Not really. There was no motivation set up beforehand. He was simply abducted. After the poem, the story went into a thick babble about consciousness only being possible when the minimal set of neuronal events and mechanisms sufficient for neural correlates of consciousness exist. Tia sighed. She did not have an inkling as to what a neural correlate was. She read the section again. The section would have lost her, except this time there was something she recognized beneath the scientific mumbo jumbo. She thought about what Bill said about bioinformatics and the fields of transgenic plants, and what Doctor Cain said at dinner the night Kay told her she was going to connect with Hugh, something about math and patterns. She highlighted the term *'neural correlates of consciousness'* and then tapped the screen. A word bubble popped up above the text.

Neural Correlates of Consciousness - A neural state that directly correlates with a conscious state, or which directly generates consciousness.

Tia tapped the screen so the bubble would disappear and read the section again. She never heard Kay speak that way. Kay was no more of a scientist than she was. Slowly, she began to piece it together. Then she understood. The clone brains could compute, they were neurons, but they couldn't be conscious. The brains needed the minimal set of neuronal events that constituted the neural correlates of consciousness to turn their consciousness on. They needed a human, a spark, a ghost in the machine.

Kay didn't ever write this way, but Tia sensed she wrote this for a reason. Kay was sending her a message.

Tia flipped back to the poem, the strange nonsensical poem. Her teeth clenched together, punishing herself for missing it. Mind shifting, she saw the letters of the acrostic puzzle lift from the tablet. The first letter of the first word jumped out at her with the first of the second and the third.

She brought up a notepad into the corner of the screen and rapidly typed in the string of letters, and then found the spaces. When she was finished, the notepad formatted the sentence.

Tia read the line aloud.

"Tia, I'm sorry, I have to follow this path. I love you, goodbye."

A metallic taste filled her mouth and her stomach shrunk tight. She tried to pull herself from the sunken cushion of the chair but fell deeper. The tablet dropped to her lap as both of her hands flew to the arms of the huge seat, and as she heaved herself out, the device fell to the floor.

Dizziness and nausea slammed her as she stood. Her eyes darted to the bookshelves, to the corridor door, and then out through the plated window across the garden courtyard to the glass-domed home of Hugh's cube.

~*~

SIXTEEN

The corridor was a blur, fleeting past Tia while she raced toward Kay. The dizziness didn't last but a few stifled breaths. She felt lightheaded, the result of the adrenalin jolt, her head tingled with worry. The twist in her gut remained. Her heart thumped hard, pumping deep up into her neck; she could hear it.

A flicker of images, events from the past few days, flashed into her mind, re-sorted from the order they occurred. Kay's laughter in the library. Quentin at the table.

Her discussions with Kay and the doctors morphed into a single conversation, each line a piece of a greater puzzle.

"It's an illusion. The way he seems to be alive," Quentin said. "Did he ask a lot of questions?"

But this time it was Kay's voice answering from the library and not Tia.

Hugh is curious as to what I believe. He asks me lot of questions.

"Uh hum," Quentin said, "that is because he is programmed to do so."

Can you believe it? He's interested in what I think. He just keeps asking and I keep talking. Sometimes I feel like I'm gonna yap his ear off, or, well, you know, bore him at least. But he just keeps asking. Nobody has ever listened to me like Hugh does.

"It's similar to the Socratic method, though not a method of inquiry designed to teach you necessarily."

He just keeps asking.

"It helps to maintain the illusion. A lot of questions give a human the impression they are talking to a conscious sentient being."

I keep talking. Sometimes I feel like I'm gonna yap his ear off.

"For your benefit. The more questions a syn asks, the more you talk, the more endorphins released into your system, the happier you become, and you reflect that happiness."

Nobody has ever listened to me like Hugh does.

As her feet rapidly dropped down the steps of the stairwell, Tia shook her head side-to-side and muttered, "That's not Hugh." And then, to affirm herself, "Not the real Hugh." She almost stumbled as she rounded the bottom of the stairwell.

Calypso kept Odysseus on that island to make him her immortal husband.

"That's the kind of research we do in the Calypso Project."

The real Hugh was trapped inside his own head.

She launched herself through the doors of the glass corridor that bridged the manor to the rest of the compound and was blinded by the burst of pure sun reflecting off the floor's white polished tile. Tia raised her arm to block the glare, tightened her eyelids, and kept moving forward. Her braid bounced against her back as she ran full kilter. Under her breath, she spat the words, "They want to make use of your brain."

The white tiles were waxed to a high sheen, and as she rounded the corner to the next set of doors, her socked feet lost traction and slipped from beneath her. She hurdled into the transparent wall, stopping hard with a thud.

Tia winced, slipped her hand to the spot on her head that slammed against the transparent alloy. The inside of her palm was warm, sticky. She rolled her head from one side of her neck to the other and then slowly brought her gaze up to the open double doors of the greenhouse. There were four blurry figures in white coveralls walking toward her. *Syns*, she thought. She squeezed her eyes tight to correct her focus and when she opened them, there were only two.

"Are you okay?" one of them asked. A man, not a syn. She recognized the voice.

"She hit her head," said the other. A woman.

The two knelt down. The woman gently eased Tia's hand away from her head with her fingertips. "She's cut herself," she said. "What were you doing, dear?"

The woman was Zaynah. Zaynah had never spoken directly to Tia before, and now she was tending to her. Zaynah's head was adorned in an aubergine ḥijāb and she was dressed in a white coat and white slacks, not coveralls at all. The man, Hector, was also wearing a white coat and white slacks.

"Can you hear me?" Zaynah asked.

Tia blinked. "I can hear you," she said. The double doors to the greenhouse were open behind the two, and she could see movement through the windows of the next set of doors far beyond, the entrance to the dome that housed the cube. She shifted up and then, failing to realize how much she'd shocked her body, immediately sank back down.

"Whoa," Hector said. "Calm down. You whacked yourself pretty good."

Tia's eyes darted between the two. "Can you help me up?"

Zaynah shook her head. "Maybe you should wait a minute. You may have broken something."

"We should get a gurney," Hector said. Zaynah nodded.

"No," Tia yelped, "I'm fine. I can get up. Please, just help me."

Again, she struggled to find her footing, this time throwing first her forearm, and then her hand against the wall. Zaynah and Hector, surprised by her effort, each took a side to support her, and then held her upright until she was stable.

Hector was visibly disturbed. "You really should wait."

"I'm okay. Really."

The two scientists lowered their arms. "What were you running from?" Zaynah asked.

Tia peered into Zaynah's eyes, suspicious, unsure. "I have to see Kay."

Hector sucked in his cheeks and dryly repeated himself, "You should wait."

"No," Tia said. "I have to see her now." She began to move forward and the two scientists each put a hand to her shoulders to stop her.

"You need to relax," Hector said. "I'll have—"

Before he could finish his sentence Tia lunged forward. "No!" she screamed, and then ran past them. She ran through the greenhouse, thrust herself through the double doors of the dome and then continued into the cube – where she abruptly stopped.

The cube had changed from her first and only visit. The vivid imagery still played across the full screen walls, but everything else in the room was different. The large chromium circle that suspended Hugh was rolled to the side. Hugh was no longer suspended from the giant ring. He lay beneath a sheet on an inclined bed, his feet angled to the floor, his head raised to the height of the chest of the four scientists working there. Another inclined bed was beside Hugh's, angled away at forty-five degrees so that the raised heads were almost touching and the feet near the floor were far apart.

Kay was to the right, on the second bed. Her head, inches from Hugh's, was shaved and sensor pads were adhered to her scalp. Wires and tubes slipped from the sheet that draped her, attached to what, Tia could only imagine. Behind Kay, dressed in the same white coats and slacks as Zaynah and Hector, were Monica, Doctor Cain, Quentin, and Allegra. Monica and Doctor Cain were working with Hugh's cranium harness, while the bald-headed Model Seven syns that tended to the cube assisted them.

No one acknowledged her entrance.

As if invisible, she watched the scientists exchange whispers as they tinkered with the cables of the shiny gold bowl. Kay's eyes were open, and she appeared to be at peace.

~*~

SEVENTEEN

Tia understood what was happening immediately.

The words came out soft, barely audible beneath her breath. "It's a trap."

She mustered more strength and blurted aloud, "It's a trap."

The scientists briefly stopped what they were doing to look at her, gazing at the oddity of her presence, of her, the tearing, red-faced girl with blood in her hair, and then all but Allegra resumed their work.

Allegra smiled. "Tia, you really shouldn't be here right now."

"It's not Hugh. It's not Hugh!"

"What's that you're saying?" Allegra asked.

"He's trapped," Tia gasped, she was beginning to break down, "and you will be too." She was not paying attention to Allegra, nor Zaynah or Hector standing by her side. She was speaking to Kay. "You have to save him. It's just like *Organic*."

Unable to twist her neck back, Kay angled her eyes behind her to address Allegra. "It's okay," she said.

Allegra stepped up next to Kay. She kept her eyes on Tia, but spoke to Kay. "I don't understand what she's saying. What is she talking about?"

"I was wrong," Kay said. "She should be here."

Allegra nodded. "Come closer," she said. "You have a little while yet."

Tia didn't move. She heard Allegra, yet her body wasn't her own. Allegra gestured to Zaynah.

"Come," Zaynah said. She took Tia by the arm to lead her. Tia resisted, her muscles tense, her legs frozen. More was happening in the room than she could comprehend. She felt her stomach tighten and then loosen, the nausea returning.

And then another voice spoke from behind her.

Sebastian.

"It's really okay, Miss Elleron." He stepped around to stand beside her. His head vibrated lightly from the activity of all of the servos beneath his vinyl face working in concert to attempt a smile like no other he ever created. At first, her gaze did not meet his. She was locked on Hugh and Kay, trying to understand why Kay was allowing what was about to happen, but slowly she let her eyes meet the bright LEDs of Sebastian's, and his too blue eyes warmed her. Then she returned his smile.

"You're crying," he said.

She blinked, once and then twice. She hadn't realized the tears had begun to well.

"Yes," she said.

"Why?"

"Because," she said, her voice meek, "I'm scared."

"You don't have to be," he said. "Kay wants to talk to you. Will you join me by her side?"

Sebastian took a small step forward, slowly lifted his hand, and held it in front of her. Tia nodded and wrapped her hand around his. His hand was warm. As real as any human hand. She let him lead her to the space between the beds. Up close, she could see they were two metal tables. She peered at Hugh as she approached, averting her eyes from Kay. He appeared to be dreaming. His beard was wooly and full of the same fine silken grey hair that still grew above his ears, but the top of his head was bald. The scientists had taken great care in preserving him. He was so much the same as the man in the image on the tablets, the photograph on Kay's archaic print books, yet older. Creases formed on his chin, his cheeks were slightly gaunt. Even the men and women of science could not hide that he was closing in on two centuries. She wondered if the metal of the table felt cold, if Hugh felt cold, if Hugh felt at all. And that brought her thoughts back to Kay. Her eyes rode the edge of Hugh's table over to the edge of Kay's. Kay on the silver metal table. She did not appear as though she felt cold, she seemed happy.

Sebastian left Tia's side. The scientists continued their work, yet they were not in her reality. Only she and Kay remained in that moment.

"I'm sorry," Kay said. "I should have told you myself. I shouldn't have left it in the story."

"Told me what?"

"Hugh is old, he is dying."

"He is a prisoner," Tia said. "You told me in the story. He was abducted."

"No," Kay raised her brow, "Honey, did you think…? Oh, you misunderstood. He was chosen, he volunteered."

"How can you know that?"

"He told me, of course."

"But that's not Hugh, that's the avatar, an AI, like Sebastian."

"No," Kay said.

"He just asks questions to fool you, like Sebastian.

That's what he's programmed to do. The Archive writes the books. Don't you see?"

"No, he asks questions because he has not left the island in so long. Sebastian asks because he cannot feel the outside world, Hugh feels the world with every plant in the forest outside."

"What do you mean? Feels the world? This is wrong."

"He's tired. He needs me to carry the torch. The waves roll in and the waves roll out, on through eternity. I'm the next wave."

"What does that even mean?"

"I'm the next wave. All of the books, almost all of them, are written here. The bioinformatics system composes most of the stories, but they need an additional element."

"Just like in your story?"

"Yes. They need the artist. There has always been a creator. There were others before Hugh. There will be others after me. These scientists of Calypso have dedicated their careers to perpetuating culture and society."

"Literary culture? Is there such a thing? No one even cares to read real writers."

"Not literary culture, our society as a whole, influencing how people think and see the world."

"Calypso. You told me she held that man captive."

"It's a clever joke, from the first author. Before Hugh. But the word really means *'concealing the knowledge'*. Calypso hides the secret to the Archive, to the Libraries."

"But why you? Why does it have to be you?"

Quentin joined Allegra and spoke, "As Kay mentioned, Hugh isn't the first. There were others before him, all noble pioneers. They told the world they had set off to sail the seas and then came here to write. Then they passed the torch as they, each in turn, realized that their bodies had become an impediment to their work. They decided to *drop their bodies* to continue their research and writing."

"So where are the others?" Tia asked.

"In there," Allegra gestured to the vid screens, "with him."

"You have to have an author," Kay said. "The Archive can customize a story, but the Archive can't come up with anything so original."

Tia raised her brow. "But isn't that exactly what Quentin said? That Hugh is a bioinformatic system, he *is* the Archive, the Archive is *him*. You've been speaking to an Avatar."

Kay's grin faltered. She peered at Tia and then slowly shifted her gaze up to Quentin.

"So is it him, or the Archive?" Tia asked.

"Well," Quentin said. "Hugh has evolved. The author as you think of him is obsolete. Miss Elleron," Quentin sighed, "one of your father's systems can write a novel in seconds. You need only adjust the algorithm. That's what we research here. We analyze what people read, what they like to read, what keeps them happy, calm, subdued."

"But you said he is writing."

"Yes, well there is one element that a bioinformatic system alone cannot duplicate. Hugh supplies that. The Archive can add all of the tropes, the romance, the conflict, and like the syns, the Archive can imitate. What is missing are the neural correlates of consciousness that constitute the minimal set of neuronal events and mechanisms sufficient for a specific conscious experience."

The neural correlates, like in Kay's story. Tia now

understood where Kay learned about them and what, at least in the simplest form, they were. "You need a human brain."

"You see, the Archive can duplicate the human ability to conceive of agency, can create agency, yet it cannot intuitively understand the power and influence of agency on a human."

"Agency? What's agency?"

"Uh... Yes, well, the Archive can come up with a character on its own, an agent, a hero, a villain, a plot, the same way a person can. All the ingredients are there, if you will. What the Archive cannot do is predict how that hero, that story, will affect the individual reader. Approximations are made, psychological predictions, yet there is no precision in the outcome. To the Archive, a flashlight will always be a flashlight. It was never the magic of the past, always the science of today. The Archive has no way of knowing when the scientist becomes the magician, or when the magician becomes the witch. The Archive can mimic the words an author would create, yet has no bearing on how those scenes affect the individual."

"So that's why you need a human?"

"Specifically, we need an author such as Hugh, because only he can add the philosophy, measured with..." Quentin pulled his lips tight, nodded and then corrected himself, "tempered with compassion. Because you see, we have discovered that people will not read stories without..." he raised his hands open palmed, "heart."

"But why Kay? Why does it have to be Kay? Because we happened to come ashore?"

From the back wall, Hugh's image filled the screen, and his voice filled the room. "I'm sorry we misled you, Tia. You did not just happen to come ashore. I," his eyes flashed across the six scientists in the room, "we, have been following Kay's work for quite some time. She is a talented author, a great author. Not only does she have the creativity of an artist and the heart of a philosopher, she has a compassion for humanity. Stories can be reduced to taxonomy, the archetype and structure you studied at the university. There are so many tropes. These are vehicles to be driven by the philosophical mind, to bring to challenge the occurrences society becomes accustomed to, so that every day the ordinary comes into question."

Tia was at a loss for what to say or how to answer.

Hugh continued, "Kay tells me you take photographs with an old camera your father gave you."

Tia nodded.

"What does the analog photograph capture that any observation camera does not?"

"My moment?"

"Your humanity, your heart and mind, and all within the confines of a frame. A photograph, a painting, both are observed in frames. Music, jazz, which has survived since before I was here, the best parts are within a framework, the music between the bars. Stories are the same. Creativity is at its highest, and the story best told when revealed within the limits of a frame. The structures, archetypes, and tropes add to culture in ensemble. Everything framed. Stories are no different. They have a beginning and an end. I, too, am framed. Through my life I've had many chapters, student, ship's captain, author, son, husband…" Hugh's eyes dropped away from Tia and the imagery running on the sidewall screens briefly, yet noticeably, slowed. He was remembering something, and then as quickly, he caught himself and the imagery on the walls resumed, and his eyes again met hers.

"Through my work I have traveled space and time, and now, framed on each side, this chapter of my story is about to end. Kay's will continue."

"No. No," Tia said. "I love her. I need her."

"The world needs her, too," Hugh said. "This is a sacrifice. For her, and for you."

"You don't understand," Kay said. "I was born for this. And I'm not going away. Not really. I will always be," she bit her lip and then added, "in the words."

"It's time," Allegra said.

Tia glanced up at the older woman. Allegra's dark eyes were a mix of kindness and sincerity.

"Okay," Kay said. "Are you ready, Hugh?"

"Yes."

Tia looked at each of the scientists in turn and then back to Allegra. "What's going to happen now?"

"The harness will be moved to Kay."

"And Hugh?"

"I will be with her," Hugh said. "Though no longer as myself."

"But your body…"

"I left that body long ago."

The urge to pull Kay from the table was overpowering.

To grab her arm and drag her willingly or unwillingly out of the cube, through the manor, and straight down to the boat.

But Tia couldn't do it.

Not because she lacked the will or the strength, or the courage. Rather because Kay was right. This was her destiny, her place in the world. Kay was not trapped on the table, the outside world was her trap. If Tia were to force her one true love away from this – all of this – she scanned the moving imagery on the wall in an effort to fathom what this really was, if she were to take Kay from this opportunity, she would be condemning her to a life of regret and unhappiness.

Her eyes again began to well, and then with an uncontrollable sob, a tear streamed from each eye. She slid her hand down onto one of Kay's round apple cheeks, and rubbed it in a soft, gentle circle. "You had such beautiful hair. You hated it, but it was so beautiful. You're so beautiful." She sobbed again, unable to hold it in, unable to stay strong for Kay. "I love you so much."

Kay's forehead softened, and her eyes, clear before, reddened at the sight of Tia's pain. "I love you too."

Tia brought the back of her other hand up across the bridge of her nose and then wiped the sides of her cheeks, blushing them further than they already were. "This is why you said goodbye the way you did."

Kay nodded. "Just kiss me."

And Tia did, softly, gently, and she focused as hard as she could on the feel of Kay's lips against hers, so that in the latest of nights or the darkest of hours, she would have that memory.

When she lifted her head, her face held the mask Kay needed to see, the one that she would leave her with. And she saw the mask reflected in Kay's, the face of a strong young woman, ready to take on the challenge of a frontier only a chosen handful of artists had ventured to before.

From her left, Tia heard a hiss and turned to see the golden cranial cap slipping from Hugh's skull. Her eyes darted up toward the side walls and then to the back wall. A circular space station hung in the orbit of an orange moon on the wall to the right, a serene oceanscape filled the left, but on the back wall, Hugh's avatar was gone. She looked at Allegra. "Is Hugh..." She let her gaze fall back onto the quiet body, inches from her, a pleasant smile appeared to creep across Hugh's face. The man that had lived so many lives, and that affected so many, that influenced the cultural evolution of nations, was now... She hesitated.

"Is Hugh dead?"

"Yes," Allegra said. "As you may describe it. But he will never be really. His patterns are forever ingrained in the bioinformatics fields, a drop in a pond, a consciousness that Kay will now guide in the collective."

"He will be in the words," Kay said. "With me."

~*~

EIGHTEEN

Sebastian kept the pace slow as he led Allegra and Tia down to the lagoon. The forest canopy and ocean beyond took on new hues of life with the coming of the sun, yet seeing past the grey that hovered over the island the duration of her stay was hard for Tia. Her mind was preoccupied. Out in the warmth and brightness of the day, the blues were bluer, the greens greener. Her camera was out, yet her heart was not into snapping pictures. Even though she told herself that she understood Kay's desire, Kay's decision, her heart was not at ease. Understanding somehow made the ache worse.

"How did you know?" she asked.

"Know what, my dear?" Allegra's face was full of grace, nurturing. The sun made her silver hair white, and though her dark eyes were hidden beneath large black sunglasses, Tia sensed her eyes were sympathetic.

"How did you know that Kay was the right one? I mean, not only as a writer, I get that. I'm sure flags were raised with her academic awards and she's in the Archive, but how did you know she would come?"

"The Librarian," Allegra said. "I mean, we didn't really know, but the Librarian did, he knew for sure."

"How do you know the Librarian?"

"We know all of the Librarians. The Libraries are part of the Calypso Project. They are essential for the Archive's higher function. To ensure the stories get into the right hands."

"But anybody can download a story, and the Archive profiles everyone's activity. I mean, isn't that how it works?"

"Oh," Allegra's mouth curved into a serious frown. "Yes and no. The Librarians are there to offer guidance, to help interpret."

"My father has a private Librarian."

"Yes... Yes, he does. Marcus Abernathy."

The magnitude was not lost on Tia. Hugh said that the reason Kay was chosen was due to her ability to influence culture and society. A society influenced by books. That only worked if they were read, if someone was there to make sure they were read. She thought about her trips abroad with her father, and her stays at the embassies in Paris, and in Prague, the printed books in the private Libraries, the Librarians. In the heavily populated world, near devoid of resources, the Librarians were essentially guiding societies conscience, and the Author, hooked up to that island sized bioinformatic system, their hidden philosopher king.

"The Author", she thought, *"Kay"*.

"We were going to sail away," she said abruptly.

"And she will," Allegra said. "Kay is in a line of many."

"Yes, Hugh said that. Hugh sailed away and he wasn't the first."

"The first to sail was an extraordinary man, he was an author, an inventor, a visionary," Allegra nodded, "he had a vision. He came up with Calypso. The technology has improved greatly since then, and others have followed, all part of the bioinformatic system, the pond."

"How will you know when Kay is..." Tia didn't know how to finish what she was asking.

"Look closely around you," Allegra said. "I believe... I believe the transition is going along just fine."

To the side of the steps, as if automated, a green sprout arose from the ground, and from its tip swelled a bud that then bloomed into a fully formed fuchsia-colored flower. A transformation that should have taken days occurred in a mere instant. Beside it, another sprout shot from the ground, and from that sprout came a bloom, then another, and another. More and more flowers began to rapidly sprout on either side of the wooden steps and then spread in a cascading wave of fuchsia and indigo across the floor of the rainforest.

A tear ran down Tia's cheek.

It was Kay.

Tia was invited to stay longer, as long as she liked, but she chose to leave a few days after Kay *'went to sleep'.'*

The scientists thought it a good idea for her to be near Kay's side during what they called *'the transition'*, yet the thought of seeing her suspended from the huge chromium ring was more than Tia could bear. So she only remained while Kay was still on the table, acclimating to the bioinformatic systems that flowed among the transgenic fields. She thought she may have liked to see Kay's avatar, then again, that may have been too much. The idea of Kay shifting to an extended consciousness was still too much, and it was better to tell herself that Kay *'was sleeping'*, that she was dreaming up new stories that were going to be shared, would inspire readers and writers, influence culture and society.

It was easier to tell herself that Kay *'went to sleep'*, and that she was still there when she needed her, when she was missing her too much, or the pain was particularly unbearable, she would read, and Kay would be beside her, with her, always. It was during those times that she truly understood her sacrifice.

For Kay was in the words.

~*~

THE
END

~*~

A NOTE FROM THE AUTHOR

Thank you for reading *Hugh Howey Lives*. This story came about after Hugh wrote a blog entry in early November 2014 titled 'Humans Need Not Apply'. In the article and the lengthy comment conversation that followed, Hugh speculated that within 100 years, computers would be writing novels and authors could be obsolete.

I emailed Hugh a pitch with a different speculation, and that is the story in *Hugh Howey Lives*.

People have asked me if I know Hugh Howey. The answer is no, I don't. Hugh allowed me to use his name in the story he inspired. We are not close friends that share emails or other correspondence. I have yet to meet him (though maybe I will one day when he visits Manhattan). In a broader sense though, Hugh is a friend to many authors, particularly freelance and indie, but not just them. He has taken time to share his experience and insights on his blog, at mentor workshops, and has famously been a pivotal inspiration in the evolving publishing industry. Because Hugh shared his experience, I connected with my editor Crystal Watanabe, and the cover artist of this book, Ben Adams. I advise anyone, writer or reader, to visit his website hughhowey.com.

If you visit Hugh's site you will notice that he sails. There was a time in my life when I sailed and I knew Hugh did too. What I did not know was that at the same time I wrote this story, Hugh was having a catamaran built – to live on, write on, to sail away on. We'll chalk that up to serendipity.

There are numerous contributors that bring a project to completion. My family, first and foremost. A myriad of fellow authors and friends. Individually, I want to thank my lovely wife, floral designer Susan Holt. She supported the project by diligently reading the first draft through the tenth. I would also like to thank the readers that signed up as First Readers for this manuscript, as their contributions have helped me to create a better release edition. I would like to thank Hugh for the thumbs up - the story would have been the same but his inclusion as a character and name in the title added a bit of pressure that I think made the work much better. I also thank author friend Susan Kaye Quinn for helping me to improve the story by sharing insights in process and inspiring me to dig deeper, Crystal Watanabe for her editing walkthroughs and cross continental discussions concerning writer minutia, and finally, Ben Adams for the stellar cover and interior art.

If you enjoyed *Hugh Howey Lives*, I would appreciate if you would share your thoughts in a review. Reviews help other readers that may have similar interest as you decide whether this is a story they would like to read.

And again, thank you.

~*~

ABOUT THE AUTHOR

Daniel Arthur Smith is the author of the international bestsellers **THE CATHARI TREASURE, THE SOMALI DECEPTION**, and a few other novels and short stories.

He was raised in Michigan and graduated from Western Michigan University where he studied philosophy, with focus on cognitive science, meta-physics, and comparative religion. He began his career as a bartender, barista, poetry house proprietor, teacher, and then became a technologist and futurist for the Fortune 100 across the Americas and Europe.

Daniel has traveled to over 300 cities in 22 countries, residing in Los Angeles, Kalamazoo, Prague, Crete, and now writes in Manhattan where he lives with his wife and young sons.

For more information, visit danielarthursmith.com

~*~

Made in the USA
Middletown, DE
02 August 2016